Flashpoint

ALSO BY C.M. BANSCHBACH

The Dragon Keep Chronicles
Oath of the Outcast
Blood of the Seer

The Drifter Duology
Then Comes A Drifter
A Name Long Buried

Spirits' Valley Duology
Greywolf's Heart
Saber's Pride

Drax Guard: Crew Six
Flashpoint
Faultline
Conduit
Stoneheart
Shrike

Fates Defiant

FLASH POINT

DRAX GUARD: CREW SIX #1

POINT

C.M. BANSCHBACH

Flashpoint

ISBN: 979-8-9890651-1-0

Published by Campitor Press

clairembanschbach.com

Cover Design: Emilie Haney @eahcreative / eahcreative.com

Drax Guard Logo: Morlin Lorenz @thatmoonysky

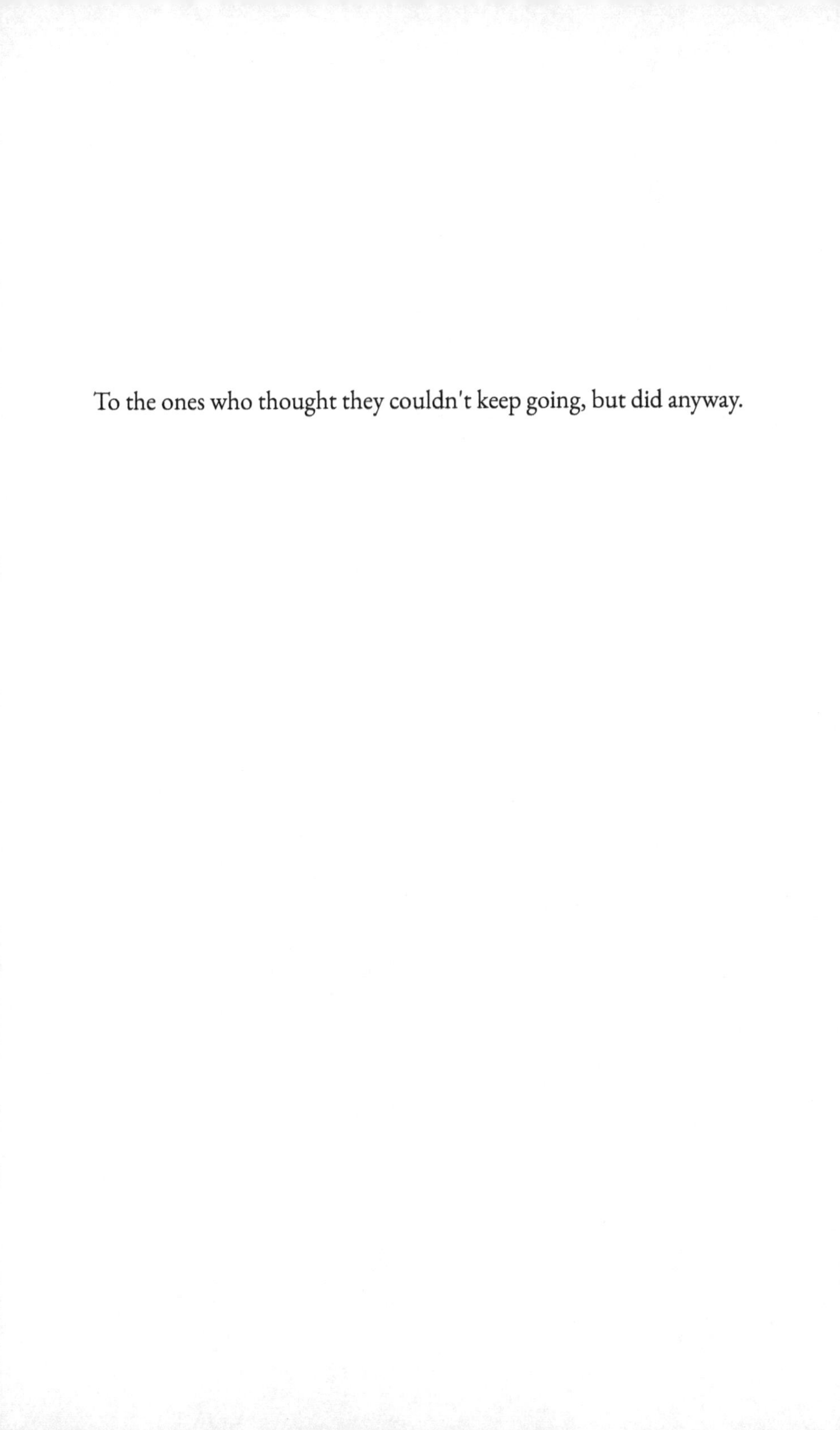

To the ones who thought they couldn't keep going, but did anyway.

1

CIERAN

WHOEVER SAID GRIEF ISN'T permanent clearly never lost anyone. It's a hole that can't be filled, and even if you start trying, something else happens to erode your progress.

At least, that's been my experience. The cold winter wind hustling around downtown Dunhare, Oregon's buildings and weaving its way through even the tiniest ingress point is not helping my general outlook. An hour ago, I executed a strategic retreat from the step of a house, unable to knock on the door. At least I dropped the birthday present on the porch.

Now, I'm on a park bench on a side of town I don't normally hit up, mostly empty coffee cup in hand, trying to find a reason to go back and at least knock on the door. Or maybe I should just keep moving and make myself tired enough to try to sleep tonight in the house that's been missing its brightest piece for four days.

My boot scuffs against the ground. A man and a woman stare at each other across the park trail. He's in a business suit, gold cufflinks catching the sunlight. Looks like he's been raised to push papers around a desk all day. She's got a tip to her ears—fae or elf, but I'm not close enough to catch the color in her eyes to tell for sure. Average height, patched jeans, and boots that look painstakingly polished. Seen a little more of life than the guy has.

They slowly move toward each other, drawn by some invisible force. If my sister were beside me, she'd be hitting my arm in excitement while I roll my eyes at seeing a heartbond activate in person. She's part of the reason I'm out here, trying to outpace her memory. Shay was only two years older than me, but cancer didn't care. It was system-wide before we even knew it was there, and some things even magic can't heal.

The newly heartbonded couple slowly approach each other, shake hands, and shyly start down the gravel path together. I turn the coffee cup in my hands and silently wish them luck, just for Shay's memory. She loved stuff like this, but I never gave it much thought. Heartbonds, soulmates. That person who makes something click into place inside you. Most people don't have one, and there's no way to know if you have one before it activates, which just sort of makes the whole thing more ridiculous.

Maybe I just don't like the idea of something being predestined. The heartbond is an instant connection and attraction that links two people so they can be stronger together. If they choose to accept it and cement it into place, they're stuck together for life. It's too much like skipping the line, finding some back door and sneaking in.

Reminds me of all the people I met in the foster system who'd try to get close with a few questions, trying to bridge the gap I held between everyone and me. Only my sister could breach it. She'd always be there in silent understanding each time someone tried to take the place of our parents or younger brother and I didn't allow it.

A silver-tufted squirrel hops closer, eyeing my almost-empty coffee cup. At some point in its short life, it must have gotten caught in some fae magic or scampered through a natural magic reservoir to get that silver streak across its ears and tail. The magic clearly hasn't affected it, except to make it even bolder than the other squirrels around, which is saying something.

Tossing back the last sip of lukewarm coffee, I sling the cup into the trashcan a few feet from the bench. The squirrel tracks the path, nose twitching, and darts away to circle the can. A chill breeze sneaks though the holes in the knees of my jeans. I tuck my hands into jacket pockets, slouching further on the bench with shoulders hunching up to my ears. A bit of weak winter sunlight slipping through the clouds does a poor job of bringing some warmth back to my skin.

Two teens kiss by the wall where they think no one can see. Children shout by the swings, and their moms are giving me some glances. They'd probably usher their kids away if they knew about the knife in my boot and the other under my jacket sleeve. But right now, I'm just the weirdo on the park bench.

A bus hums by on the nearest road. The vehicle's got a faint sputter every three seconds. Something's knocked its power crystal loose. Either no one knows how to fix it, or they haven't noticed it yet to take it to the repair shop.

A sigh cuts from me. I have no reason yet to keep going, no reason to move on. In more ways than just from this bench.

The dirt over my sister's grave is four days old. She'd left the world too early, people said. Shay was the type of person to make you feel whole, and now her absence is creating tiny craters everywhere. From the way people talked, it had been more sad that she'd never gotten married, never had kids. Like someone would be missing something they didn't even know they had.

But they hadn't seemed to care that I'd always have a part missing now, too. Another missing piece to add to the cavity of our parents and younger brother, formed when I was twelve. The gaping hole left by three other deaths who'd been brothers, family to me.

It's just me now. And maybe I have too many missing pieces for any one person or thing to fill them up. I can't even make it into a four-year-old's birthday, the one I'd promised my sister I'd go to. The kid whose father I couldn't bring home like I had so many times before. I'd just dropped a package on the damn porch.

Groaning, I pull my hands free and lean onto my knees, rubbing my eyes.

"What's eating you now?" The voice is husky, tinged with a hint of a drawl.

I straighten. I hadn't heard anyone coming, but the stocky elf now perched on the back of my bench could sneak up on a wraith.

"The usual."

"Life in general?" Ylan nods sagely, tucking hands into his leather jacket. The wind shoves his short, black hair. Like all full elves, bits of silver shoot through his dark green eyes.

I slump back. "Yeah."

"Heard about Shay." He lifts his chin to glance around the park. "Sorry."

I shrug my shoulder. "Thanks."

"How's your headspace, Cir?" His light Texas accent softens the vowels further into the *Keer* most shorten my name into. The same way he'll gently correct his name to *Elan*.

The new heartbound couple is now hand in hand on their second lap of the park. The squirrel is back, circling the bench like it might want to try to coax some magic from Ylan. But a magpie beats him to it, flapping down awkwardly to land on the bench. Ylan frees a hand from his jacket and reaches down to it, murmuring softly in the Nordic elven dialect as he brushes its injured wing. *Restore* and *nurture* are the key definitions of elven magic, and you'll often find elves in medical fields.

I scrape the heel of my boot against the ground. "Cluttered."

"You think you can unclutter?" He returns his hand to his jacket as the magpie takes off in a burst of motion, winging up to the sky in new freedom.

"Depends. Why?"

"Mission's forming up after some new intel." From the way his jaw clenches, it won't be a pleasant one. The kind that isn't given to regular enlisted soldiers. Which is exactly why he's here talking to me. We're both special forces and have known each other for years since we were just enlisted grunts in the Army. He probably volunteered to come find me.

"What kind?" I ask anyway.

He glances around again. "Got word that dragonwalkers are out and about."

I snort a laugh. Dragonwalkers live on a small independent archipelago nation off the northern coast of Africa, and they don't leave very often. And they certainly don't come this far west.

"Your source from one of the drug dens on fortieth?"

Ylan runs a squad in the deep cover division and knows a variety of interesting people. His green-and-silver eyes flicker in the sun as he leans closer. "No. A grif patrol picked up their scent and tracks out in the Wastelands."

A shudder cuts through me. The Wastelands, hundreds of miles wide and stretching nearly the length of the Allied American States. A smoky, desolate place left over from a civil war that turned Allied against a fire drake invasion. It all ended when the drakes' volcanic nest in the northwest territories was set off, then went supervolcano when its wild magic mixed with the magic thrown around in the soil and air after years of war. The eruption wiped out hundreds upon hundreds of miles of civilization and scarred the country.

"So, why come all this way to tell me?" I haven't taken a mission with the Guard in fourteen months.

"You could walk that territory blindfolded."

"I can give whatever info the CO needs to send a team."

"CO put your name up top." A bit of sympathy sneaks through his voice.

I don't want his sympathy. I want to stay outside the Wastelands.

"Why are you here? Why didn't he just call?"

Ylan gives me a pitying look. "You know you only get calls if your phone is on?"

I swallow hard. Yeah. It's been days since I've kept my phone on more than a few minutes to check messages. Months since I've responded to anything other than a direct contact from our CO. Well-wishes, check-ins, condolences, dinner invites...they've all gone unanswered for over a year.

Which is why I've got someone from deep cover sitting on my bench. I don't know if Ylan is on mission right now or if he volunteered to come find me, but it's still a pointed reminder to keep my phone on.

"Sorry I haven't been around," he says softly.

That lump resurfaces. We were in the same platoon back in the day. Before we decided to be stupid and test into the elite Drax Guard. Ylan ran a squad for a year or two before he got roped into the deep cover division. He'll vanish with his team for days or months at a time, no contact.

I jerk a nod. His hand drops on my shoulder for a second, squeezing hard. I don't have any words, don't have anything to ask how he's doing. I'm pretty sure he was crushing on Shay for as long as he'd been coming around. It seemed to end once he was in deep cover, but he'd also been around a little in the last few months once news of her diagnosis made the rounds.

"He wants you in his office in an hour." Ylan rises to his feet, hops the bench, and vanishes through a small copse of bushes.

Him not offering to come with me tells me everything. He's on mission, and I don't know when he'll resurface. I'm on my own.

One hour.

If I leave now, I'll have enough time to get home, change into a set of dark grey fatigues, and catch a ride via bus to the command center. The glint of my prosthetic catches the light through the hole in my jeans. The best elven surgeons had spliced metal to skin with magic, but they couldn't take away the phantom pain that sometimes still rears up over a year later.

Maybe I'll turn up like this, the limb visible through my off-duty clothes to remind the CO why I'm not going on this mission.

2

Cieran

It's a ten-minute bus ride to the right quadrant of Dunhare, and then another fifteen-minute brisk walk if I decide to hurry. A few hundred years ago, Dunhare was just a glorified Army camp in central Oregon, nestled in on the western side of the Cascade Mountains. The fire drake war turned it into a refugee and Allied forces camp. It was from here that a team of four soldiers struck out to hit the volcanic nest. They didn't make it back, but their legacy started the Drax Guard.

The Army base takes up the northwest quadrant of Dunhare and the Drax Guard command tower is its own section. I get through the gate checkpoint in moments, but my feet start to drag on the steps leading into the stone building. Technically, my one-hour deadline still gives me plenty of time to get up to the fourth-floor offices.

Another wind gust skids around the corner and drives me inside. My boots halt in the atrium on the mosaic replica of our sigil—a bloody fire drake coiled around a sword. *Fear No Fire* curves in bold relief underneath.

But fire destroyed the soldier who'd become a brother, and had left scars all over me.

The memorial wall rises to my left, a painted mural of the original four above it. Rows of names are etched into the marble surface and pictures are scattered around—both formal portraits and the dead with their crews. Two hundred years of names who didn't make it back from their missions.

I can't look. Haven't been able to since I set foot back in this building ten months ago, body healed, prosthetic limb cleared for return to duty, but numb to the core.

Corporal Masood Nazari

Specialist Javier Moreno

Specialist Marcel Anderson

Most days I feel like my name should be up there with them—*Sergeant Cieran O'Donnell*, but here I am instead. I don't need pictures to remember them, because my photographic memory has plenty of good times to flip through. But I've been stuck on the bloody, smoking, *helpless* moments that were seared into my brain on our last mission together. My brain has it all keyed into a slideshow, sometimes playing in cinematic slow-motion, and I can't quite get past it to any other memory.

The building guards say nothing. We acknowledge each other with a look as I hurry past, bypassing the elevators and going for the stairs instead. It's four floors and a basement sublevel, but there's always something wrong with the elevators and I'm not interested in gambling with death again by stepping inside one today.

CO's office is at the end of the hall. The door is open so he can see anything or anyone coming. At least he has the decency to not watch me every step of the way into his space.

"Ah, Cieran. We had bets going on if you were going to show." Captain Bron Wolfe, the commander of the Drax Guard, leans back in his desk chair, fingers steepling together.

He's in Drax Guard grey, insignia patch on his left shoulder, and rank bars on his collar. Bits of grey frost his dark hair, cropped in a more standard Army cut than the rest of us in the Guard. Like me, he's human with no magic, but has a well-earned reputation as a hard-ass. Combat stories still circulate even though he's been manning this position for longer than I've been in the Guard, and no one he served with is active duty anymore.

I scowl, flopping down in the chair opposite and pulling my beanie off my short hair. "Which way did Ylan bet?"

Wolfe just tilts his head, and I almost grab my phone from my jacket pocket to turn it on and text him *"shilsa"* for prodding me into coming so he'd win a bet.

"He said you needed info," I continue.

"Something like that." Wolfe flips open a report on his desk and nudges it toward me.

Annoying curiosity sends me leaning forward to pull it over and sit back to read it. My eyebrows arch higher with every sentence of the bare report. Dragonwalkers typically stay out of international politics, stay under the radar, and guard their islands and the secrets of dragons. Most natural dragons are either dead or else retreated into deep hibernation a few hundred years ago with the progressive rise of technology merging with magic. The only dragons still out and about are these dragon shifters, and that garners a lot of unwanted attention—innocent and criminal.

"They sure it's dragonwalkers?" I ask anyway. "There hasn't been any incident, has there?"

Technically, the Wastelands are a no-man's-land—part of America, but not really governed by any state. Barely livable. A fact that gangs and criminals take advantage of frequently.

He leans forward to reclaim the folder. "Not yet."

"What are you going to do about it?" I make a point to rub my right knee where the metal is visible through my jeans.

He catches the motion and smiles, but it seems to snag a little as it creases his face. "I know what you're going to say."

"Good. So we're done here?" Only my near perfect track record—and recent events—gives me the courage to talk like this.

He places his clasped hands on the desk. "Cieran. You're one of the best."

"Was." I rap knuckles against my metal knee with a hollow thud. "And you know where I got this souvenir."

Wolfe nods. The mission he'd sent me on to the Wastelands fourteen months ago had ended up in disaster. Got my squad killed, and got me carried home without the bottom half of my right leg and a few breaths short of a coffin myself. Even now, I'm a little twitchy about stepping foot outside the city. At least the sorcerer terrorist we'd been tracking is dead, and his organization in shambles. That's the only thing that gets me to sleep for a few hours at a time.

"All the docs have cleared you. The limb replacement is fit for duty. You've done multiple patrols and training exercises with the enlisted units without a problem."

I shift in my chair. *Replacement.* Makes it sound like the prosthetic is a perfect replica of my limb. Like it doesn't slow me a half beat due to the weight. Doesn't give me a slight hiccup to my gait pattern that I'll never be able to hide. Sure, it gives me a little extra heft in a kick, but getting it there is the problem.

Maybe it's just the excuse to hide behind because deep down, I am scared shitless to go back out into the barren territory.

"You're the best we've got."

"Surely some young upstart is looking to prove themselves." I pill the edge of the beanie between my fingers. I say young like I'm not twenty-eight, but ten years of serving in the western A.S.A. forces—six of those in the spec ops Drax Guard—sometimes makes me feel older.

Wolfe chuckles. "You'd have heard about it if there was. You gonna take this or make me order you?"

I sigh and rub above my eyebrow with my thumb.

"It's just a quick run. In and out. The dragonwalkers didn't appear hostile. Figure out what they're doing and then come right back."

I pause, tilting my head. "Well, it sounds so easy when you put it that way." Except there is nothing easy about the Wastelands.

But maybe this is what I need. A push out the front door to make me face my fears. Trial by fire to get my feet back under me. Drills or patrols along the A.S.-Mexican border, or even the slightly more tumultuous Yukon borderlands, are nothing to a real fight alongside the Guard.

"Okay, boss."

Bron flashes an understanding smile. "I've got a crew, or you can pick your own. Either way, I want you headed out ASAP. Grif squad will give you a lift."

"Which crew?"

"Six."

I nod. Exactly who I'd pick now that I'm a sergeant without my own crew. "Who's taking lead?"

They have their own sergeant, and I'll gladly defer to his expertise. Mostly so I don't have to be in command out there again.

Wolfe must read that loud and clear in my face, because he gives a sort of apologetic slant of his head. "Pothos took a transfer to the reserves last month, so Kostic's been filling in as squad leader."

I shift in my chair, hand tightening around the beanie in a wordless curse. But it's just a quick in and out. I can do that.

"There's a spot for a sergeant on the crew." It's left out in the open between us, and something sours in the back of my throat. Wolfe's offering me a place with a new crew if I'm ready.

My reply is focused on the mission. "I'm good with them. They already know?"

Bron nods. "Ready and waiting on confirmation that you're taking point."

"I hate you, sir," I inform him as I push to my feet. "I've got gear here. I'll be ready when that grif squad is."

The sooner I can get this over with, the better.

3

CIERAN

I PAUSE OUTSIDE THE locker room. Murmurs of conversation hum through the cracked door—the voices of my temporary crew. All soldiers I've fought alongside over the last several years. Not part of *my* squad. But I'm the only one from Crew Eight still alive.

Shoving the beanie into my jacket pocket, I push open the door and step inside. The conversation dies for a telling two seconds.

"Cir!" Besim Antilles lifts his hand in a wave.

I nod back. The hulking half-troll places his sheathed longsword across his knees. Communications Specialist, and someone you don't want to get on the bad side of because he'll guilt you with a soft look long before he pulls that sword.

"You're in?" he asks.

All trolls look like tall, bulky humans, but with a deep grey stoneskin that makes them tougher than granite. Besim's half-human side shows with dark hair and tanned skin, but he tops six-feet five, and has broad shoulders and a bulkiness to his lower jaw that shouts his heritage. He can call up that stoneskin to cover his body in combat, giving him an extra edge of protection to supplement our armor. I once saw him blank-faced crack a small stone in his teeth in front of a new recruit, then burst out laughing at the kid's horrified reaction. One of the few times I've seen Dejan laugh, too.

"Looks like it." I keep my hands in my pockets. "Everyone on board?"

Corporal Dejan Kostic, the wiry elf and crew medic, shrugs. He's incredibly snippy for a medic, quick and effective with either bow or sword, and doesn't really talk to anyone outside his team. Except maybe to piss someone off or correct their pronunciation of his name. That Slavic *j* sounds more like a *y* and he'll let you know. We get along fine after a few missions, but that first one was a doozy.

Specialist Remy Kalama tilts his chin up. With Pothos gone, he's the only warlock, a human with innate elemental based magic. Remy's a lot more friendly and easygoing than Dejan, but sticks close to the medic. They've gotten all the odd couple jokes. Besim's the buffer between them and everyone else.

I cross to my locker, spinning the tumbler until it clicks. "Pothos discharged?"

I should have known about that, should have heard something. There would've been a party. But chances are high I wouldn't have gone anyway. Can't make it to a kid's birthday party, probably wouldn't make it to a "hey, you survived so civilian life can kill you instead" party.

"Rem was giving him too many grey hairs," Dejan replies, and the punch Remy gives his shoulder is audible.

I know a few things about them all. Remy's the youngest of the crew at twenty-six, and Dejan's the oldest somewhere in his forties, but he's an elf with a two-hundred-year life expectancy so maturity-wise, he's somewhere between Remy and my age. Besim's got a year on me, maybe, but the wisdom of an ancient. Everyone knows you can go talk to Besim about anything and he'll give you an answer. It's usually "go to *firren* therapy" except he doesn't curse.

"Said it was time." Besim says the words carefully and there's a clenching in my chest. Maybe they think I should have taken the discharge too. "Wanted to patch things with his wife, see his kids. He went reserves last month."

"Working a desk job." There's distaste in Dejan's tone that I feel.

He's got a clipped edge to his accent from somewhere up north, maybe even the Vinland province on the other side of the border that sometimes comes through even when he speaks the Slavic elf dialect. But he doesn't talk about himself. Not outside his crew anyway. It's a much more personal relationship between crew members, usually who've gone through Hell Week together and been in a squad since. It pummels my stomach again, thinking of the bonds I lost.

I glance over my shoulder. "How long you think he'll last?"

They chuckle.

"Surprised he didn't try to get himself put back on this mission." A faint awkwardness follows Besim's comment. If Pothos were here, it would mean I wouldn't be, and wouldn't have to walk out into the Wastelands in charge of another mission.

Remy rescues the silence. "You hear what we're tracking?" He's three-quarters native Hawaiian and has a hefty dose of the wildfire magic the human islanders are gifted with, thanks to the proximity to the magma dragons now sleeping deep in the earth's core. He's a quiet guy, so you'd never guess he's one of the most powerful warlocks we have in the Guard. Besides the magic, he's quick with the sword on his left, and the short sword with basalt inlaid in the fuller that he's burnishing right now. The blade helps him channel and harness his magic for his wide range of combat spells. I think he has a kid, too.

"Dragonwalkers," I reply. "Told the boss he sounded crazy."

Dejan snorts and starts sorting through his arrows. "And we're sure the grif squad wasn't on something?"

I shuck my jacket and shirt, pulling out a long sleeve thermal to replace it. The conversation doesn't die the way it does with some of the enlisted soldiers when the ropy burn scars along my side and back show for a few seconds. The rescue squad had found me too late for the surgeons to do much for the wild magic burns except treat the wounds, and later keep the scars from contracting and limiting movement.

"Think this is them trying to get us back for the Gulf mission?" Besim chuckles as he rolls the sleeves of his thick shirt up to his elbows and straps on forearm bracers over his mail shirt.

Low laughs answer. I don't. Because I hadn't been on that mission. I've been steering clear of anything remotely spec ops, instead slumming it with the enlisted soldiers on some easy, routine patrols. Something I've gotten looks for from others in the Guard.

My boots and jeans go into the locker, replaced with thicker combat trousers, and heavy calf-high boots.

Long-sleeved armored shirt next. It has twice the resistance as old-school chain mail, a quarter the weight, and none of the jingle. It feels like a rougher, thicker thermal. But for some reason the wizard developers didn't want to get rid of the shine. What you get when you put magic users with a couple degrees each and a superiority complex in charge of anything. I throw on a hooded jacket to cover the shine and ward against the cold and damp plaguing the Wastelands.

Heavier tac vest last, weighted front and back by concealed armored plates etched in some basic protective wards. They'll reduce the chance of sudden impalement and take the edge off common attack spells. Last are my sunglasses tucked into a strap on the vest's front.

The small mirror in the back of the locker door shows at least the head and shoulders of a Drax Guard. One who looks a little sick to his stomach. Dark circles line my hazel eyes, thick hair a little rowdy from the beanie.

At twelve, I'd have punched anyone who said I looked like my sister, but now it's punching *me* how much we grew to resemble each other. Shay and I both got the narrower face from our mom, but I got the bit of square jaw from Dad. She was nagging me from her literal death bed about how haggard I've been looking. Food and sleep have been fluctuating priorities for the last fourteen months.

My ident tags press cold against my chest under the layers. The weight helps fill up one of the missing pieces plaguing me since the last trip to the Wastelands.

I reach into the back corner of the locker and pull out the broadsword with a leather-wrapped hilt perfectly worn to my hand. It's stayed there for months. I've used one of my Army-issued spares for any missions or trainings since, but it doesn't feel right going out without my main weapon.

The blade was a gift when I made it into the Guard from the foster parents who connected the most with me and Shay. I lived with them from sixteen to eighteen. The guy had been a gruff former soldier who'd set me straight about a lot of things and felt like having a dad again. Dave Sheridan is the main reason I enlisted in the Army. Shay and I joked that if it wasn't the Army, I'd likely be in jail. It's probably not far off.

I've been dodging his calls too.

I set the sword on the bench and pull out the knife box, selecting four—one smaller for my boot, a hunting knife on the front of the vest, one in the back of my belt, and the other on my right thigh.

Straddling the bench, I set to work sharpening the blades. The others keep light conversation around me. I can feel the glances they cast to me, questioning my headspace the way Ylan had. Wondering if I'm really set and ready to go. CO is sending me one way or another, so guess I have to be.

"Cir." Besim's rumble finally brings my head up from my work. "Heard about your sister. Sorry." He tips his head.

My hand tightens around the hilt. I manage a nod.

"Good to go out today?" Dejan leans forward on his knees, light silver-green eyes watching me intently. He's covered his mail shirt with a high-collared black thermal under his armored vest.

The look on his narrow face mirrors Remy's. Not so hidden in Besim's blocky features.

For soldiers like us, death is a part of living, part of the job. But no one really bothers to see how much it affects us. As long as the Drax Guard can still walk, they can still be sent out.

We're the gatekeepers of insanity for each other.

I slide a cloth down the blade. "CO asked me to do this job. I'm in for it, and I'm clear to go."

"You sticking around after?" Remy turns a knife over in his hands. He wears the short-sleeved grey under his tac vest, but has buffed the mail shirt with something darker to hide the shine. His fire magic will keep him warm no matter the cold.

Sticking around with the Guard again. I sheathe my sword with a snap and stand to belt it around my waist. "We'll see when we get back."

Dejan frowns. He pushes up and grabs a dark ballcap to settle backwards over pale blond hair, further highlighting the tips of his pointed ears. He's not saying anything. Yet.

I grab my pack and a ballcap from the locker before slamming it shut. "I'll meet you outside."

My steps pause three strides down the hall, and I stare at the hat I grabbed without thinking. Dull grey, mottled with old sweat stains from countless missions, fraying a little around the bill. Well-worn in and sturdy with a small *staying* charm and a *"So you stop losing your hat more than anyone I know, Sarge,"* from Marcel.

I don't want to go back in just to get a different one. I jam the hat backwards on my head and keep moving. A slightly heavier thud on the prosthetic side marks my stride down the linoleum hall to the quarter-master.

"Cieran!" The dwarf looks up in surprise.

"Hey, Emma." I plunk the pack down on the table.

Quartermaster Emma Myerson eyes me up and down, taking in my dark grey fatigues and vest insignia, which matches the Drax Guard patch on her right sleeve. Her rusty red hair is tucked in a neat bun, and you're in serious trouble if she pulls out her glasses. You bust gear and you answer to her. Even our grif squad division runs scared.

"Haven't seen you in here in a minute." She crosses her arms over her chest.

My throat tightens up. "Yeah, well, been busy."

"What's getting you back out with some real soldiers?"

"CO wants me to help check out the newest report coming from the Wastelands."

She arches a red eyebrow. "The dragonwalker sighting?"

I force a smile and a shrug. "Yeah. Go out, make sure the grif squad needs their eyes checked, get back. Easy, right?"

Emma huffs bare amusement. "You sure you're up for that?"

"As sure as the last five times I answered that question today," I say through clenched teeth.

Her eyebrow stays cocked. "All right."

She begins to pull ration packs and equipment from the shelves behind her. I pack them in alongside my spare set of thermals and trousers. A longer tube of shiny material hooks into straps on the back. Fae-developed bedroll—takes up barely any space, but manages to be comfortable and adapts to external temperature. Much better than the bulky bedrolls from basic that the foot soldiers still have to use. Perks of being in spec ops.

She holds one more thing out. A two-inch-wide wristband.

"Figured you might need a new one." This time her voice quiets a little. The raised bench she stands on gives her enough height over the table for her gaze to slide down to my right leg. I take the band and buckle it on my left wrist above my watch.

"Any updates?" I ask.

"The boys finally fiddled out a smoother release for it. And upgraded the waterproofing." She lifts her chin in an invitation to test it.

I step back for more room and tap the raised circle in the middle of the band. A round shield bursts out, sections forming and melding together. Habit sends my hand into the grip.

"Well?" she asks.

I check the dulled surface of the shield and the warding runes etched around the rim. Unlike wizards who like the warrior aesthetic, dwarf craftsmen still understand the value of making a piece of equipment actually work for the soldier.

A tap to the underside of the band sends the shield whirling back into the compartment.

"Looks good."

"You'd say that about a cabbage." She shakes her head.

A bit of a grin threatens. "Comms?"

Emma hands over the earpiece and receiver, adding a few more things to my pack as I hook it into my ear and to my vest.

"Give these to Kalama." She plunks two chocolate bars on the counter. "He doesn't like fae crafted, and we just got in a shipment of the elf-made stuff."

I stick the bars into a thigh pocket until I can hand them off to Remy. All magic users carry chocolate around. Something about it helps kickstart an immediate recovery if they use too much magic, or don't set a spell right and get drained.

"Good luck out there, Cir."

I shoulder the pack, shrugging against the weight.

"Thanks, Em," I say, and head out.

The others wait on the roof with the grif squad, four men in the tan fatigues of the Army air support teams. They'll shift into two-ton griffins as soon as we're ready to go. Wolfe stands a little apart. All eyes turn to me as I step out. The ten strides to join them at the edge of the roof seem like a mile. Hooking a hand into the collar of the armored vest, I go to stand with the squad.

I hand the chocolate to Remy. He checks the label and nods before undoing a pocket on his vest and switching out chocolate. Dejan rolls his eyes and takes what must be fae made and sticks it in one of his vest pockets. Medics keep extra bars around too, and I'm a little relieved to see the backup stash for both of them. Remy just shrugs.

After a successful comm check initiated by Besim, Wolfe turns to me. "All set, Sergeant?"

He uses my rank as if to remind me one more time that I'm the one responsible for whatever happens out there. Like the sickening thought hasn't been running nonstop in the back of my head since I left his office.

"Yes, sir. You have the rundown?"

He extends the papers and my temporary squad circles up to look over them with me.

Four dragonwalkers, if that's what the blurry aerial photos could claim, walking in humanoid form across the torn hills. Other photos give landmarks and a few more shots of the dragonwalkers in different locations. One barely confirms the claim—a winged lizard-like shape jumping over the landscape.

"Grif squad will be back at the drop point in four days. Don't engage the dragonwalkers unless hostile. Get some info, keep the peace, and get back in one piece." Wolfe nods as if it's nothing more than a walk around the main street gardens—all neatly curated and full of cuddly squirrels.

A breeze sneaks down the collar of my hooded jacket, somehow making it past the layers to shudder down my back.

"Yes, sir," I manage along with the others.

The grif squad begins rolling their shoulders and tilting their heads side to side. They spread out along the edge of the roof. We step back to allow the nearly seven-foot shifters room to exchange their golden-brown skin for lithe winged-lion bodies. The eyes stay the same—gold, sharp, cat-like peering out from the eagle head.

We're flying out to keep this low profile instead of using a portal gate or transfer circle. Those are harder over long distances and might as well send up a signal letting the entire area know we're there.

The squad leader flaps his wings, uttering the clear note to signal us.

"Stay sharp," Bron calls, stepping back farther as we each head to a griffin. I grab the straps around my ride's shoulder and haul myself up onto his back, lying flat on my stomach and hooking arms and hands through the straps.

Two quick pats to his shoulder and the griffin crouches on the edge of the roof. My stomach flips uncomfortably. Last time I did this, I'd walked with a bit more swagger and had just shared a laugh with Javi.

The griffin spreads wings, and I can feel his entire body coiling and tensing. I close my eyes, squeezing the straps in a white-knuckled grip.

A burst of air against my face, a drop in my stomach at the sudden weightlessness, then the rush of wings powering up, up, up, to gain altitude.

Eventually, another shriek sounds. I open my eyes to see bits of cloud rushing by. I sit up, scooting closer to the straps to hook my legs in and leave arms free if I want.

Dunhare falls behind as we head east. Patchwork farmland spreads out as dark squares prepped for winter, giving way to low mountains and rivers. We cross through a gap between peaks, and eastern Oregon with its plains flashes underneath. An hour later, the grif squad angles southeast, leaving the "civilized" states and territories behind.

A few more towns huddle on the earth's surface. They disappear into the distance. The crumbled and broken wall of what used to be another mountain range of proud, rocky peaks comes into view. My stomach falls to earth.

The Wastelands.

From hundreds of feet in the air, the ragged hills spread out for miles, falling over the curve of the horizon. The earth keeps a scorched darkness, even though the war was over two hundred years ago. Twisted trees and jagged rock formations crop up in clusters. No rhyme or reason to it, just pushing up wherever they can through the burned crust.

It's a place you expect to see skeletons grinning around every corner. Instead, there are only swirls of mist curling up from the earth as if fires still burn beneath the soil. Drug runners and criminals find plenty of reason to hide out here from the law. I've even run across a few enterprising groups of trolls and dwarves establishing civilization out in the hills to try to get to the mineral deposits under the surface. Both have affinity for stone and crafting...if they can get along for long enough to work together.

A chirping signal prompts me to loop my hands back through the straps. I tuck my head down between my hands, pressing close to avoid the wind from the descent. All too soon, the griffin's claws settle on the ground with a crunch. I stare at my gloved hands shaking around the straps and swallow dryness in my mouth. The griffin twists to look at me with a sharp eye.

I slide off, eyes squeezing shut as my boots hit the ground.

I can get through this. I steady my sword at my side and jog the few steps to clear the space for the grif squad to take off. They'll wait just outside the Wastelands to reduce attention and the potential for them to get attacked by whatever or whoever is around.

The grif sergeant dips his head, then the squad launches into the air. Leaving us alone and completely stuck in the stupid, *firren* Wastelands.

4

Cieran

Dejan resettles his cap, still backwards like mine, and tugs the strap of his quiver. Remy slides his short sword in and out of the holder on his back, checking the release before doing the same to the second sword buckled on his left side. Besim and I do the same, checking equipment, making sure we're ready for our first step out.

Besim pulls a tablet from his vest, then shakes his head. It's what we all already know. Whatever magic still hums through here wreaks havoc on electronics and any long-range communication. But our short-range comms will be fine, reinforced with magic dampeners to withstand interference. Same with a smaller, hand-held radio he'll use to reach the grif squad if anything goes wrong before we get to the rendezvous in four days.

Dejan strings his carbon fiber bow—able to withstand the strain of being strung all day—and nods.

Hell.

"Let's get this over with." I push my sunglasses on against the dull glare from the clouds and head out.

They fall into a loose diamond pattern behind me, Dejan and his bow taking rear. Boots crunch quietly across the ground as we step around bits of broken branches or fallen trees that couldn't stay upright in the ashy soil.

I track east and a little north, heading towards one of the easier paths already slashed through the Wastelands. A constant, low-level wind cuts across the tops of the hills, stirring the smoke and kicking up slender dust devils until they spin out. The sound keeps one foot hovering over the edge, and tension ridges my shoulders trying to keep me from falling apart on the path.

The day passes with one foot in front of the other, small breaks for sparing sips of water, silently watching the hills around us. Every now and then, I stop and pull out my map, comparing the memories I really want to stay buried with the info we got from the grif squad.

Still headed the right direction.

They don't say anything, which means the mask I've got on is working. Because inside is bloody panic with every step. I can't breathe, and it's not the dust.

Sunset is a fiery red ball sinking lower and lower through the bare bones of the trees and the never-ending haze of dust. Remy heads off farther into the hills as we stop again. Nothing passes between us except glances my direction. Trying to see if my head is still on straight.

"Found a spot, Sarge." Remy's voice cuts through the comms, the suddenness of it accelerating my heartrate. I shift, covering how much it startled me. Another check to weapons and we all push off again, following the directions he gives. Five minutes later, we're setting up camp in a hollowed-out dell off the track. Several trees loom over the opening, giving some shelter from the night creeping in.

They all share a look.

"I'll take first watch," Besim offers.

Remy takes the next. Dejan just tilts his head up. He's got third watch. Which means I'm last. Reaping the benefit of hours of uninterrupted sleep.

Joke's on them, because I haven't slept through the night since the hospital discharged me and kept their drugs to themselves. But it's a nice gesture. They recognize how crappy this whole deal is for me. Like I said, gatekeepers for each other.

I just really hope I don't snap all over them.

———

Dawn sneaks up on me where I'm sheltered at the roots of the biggest tree. Quiet night. Quieter morning.

There aren't birds to greet the sun each morning. Not like the sparrows who live outside my sister's window. Or the window of whoever is going to buy the house once I give permission to the realtor to put it on the market when I get back.

The thought makes me tuck my hands deeper under my arms. I'd crashed at Shay's place once out of the hospital, not really wanting to go back to my quiet apartment. Then came her diagnosis. Then it never really seemed like a good time to officially move out and find a new apartment to lease. I'd hate to see it and the light blue window trim and little herb garden under the kitchen window go.

It felt like home with the two of us there.

A grunt and quiet muttering brings my attention back to the dell. Remy is up and swinging his arms to loosen them up from a night on the ground. Even fae bedrolls don't take away all the discomfort from Wastelands camping trips. Besim sits across the hollow from me, eyes closed, and fingers sliding over a rosary. I swallow hard. Shay had found religion years ago and kept the prayer beads around. But I've never been able to take that step myself with the way life keeps piling on.

One more check to the surrounding hills, then I slide down into the dell and start packing up. I choke down a few bites of a tasteless protein bar, and we are on the way again.

We take up the same formation as the day before, alternating every few hours who's in the lead. Lunch is what passes for some sort of Asian fusion—rice and mystery meat in an even more mysterious red sauce once you add water to the pouch. We stand or crouch as we eat. My weight is fully shifted off my right leg, giving it a few minutes of relief after the miles it's not quite used to.

"Tell you one thing." I stab at a piece of what I hope is meat. "Didn't miss these."

It gets a chuckle or two.

"You'd think with the equipment we have, they'd figure out how to make better ration packs." Besim scoops a spoonful of rice.

"Food should be first priority," Remy agrees. "When this is done, Sarge, you're coming over with the guys, and I'm making a real hot pot meal."

The others perk up at this. I manage a smile while the food officially loses all taste. My old crew didn't have a cook like Remy, but there was an all-day breakfast place we'd hit up morning after a mission. Staff knew us all. They comped the first round of waffles and bacon every time.

I haven't been back in fourteen months. Can't stomach the taste of real breakfast food. My sister got used to me just having a cup of coffee no matter how tempting the food looked.

I glance up and see the crew are all watching me again. Dejan casually goes back to stabbing his fork into his pouch. Remy folds his over and buries it. Food sucks, but the packaging is biodegradable thanks to the fae environmentalists in the supplies division. Fae draw their magic right from nature like sponges. They're basically refineries for the wild magic, taming it from its sometimes-volatile form with ancient Gaelic words or spell-casting forms. It makes them the most powerful magic users, so they're pretty invested in keeping the world healthy. But I don't think it's going to help the Wastelands that much.

"If you need to talk about anything, Sarge, we're here to listen," Besim says carefully.

You'd think a guy like him who inherited more of the physical troll traits from his dad would be all about fighting and winning. But I've seen him get a grown man crying with a few kindly words after a rough mission.

His words send my hand clenching. "What I *need* is to get this done, get out of here, and then back to doing whatever next step the therapist thinks will get my life back on track. Like I've hit a minor bump in the road, and it didn't get blown completely to hell fourteen months ago."

I dump my ration pouch and yank my pack back on, walking away a few feet to try to gather a breath and wait for the others to finish.

I don't need a new crew, or new relationships. What I need is to rewind, go back to that mission, make better decisions. Get it right so I'm not the only one left standing with my mistakes anymore.

I force my hands to unclench from around my pack straps. I also need to make sure I'm not a complete *shilsa* right now. It's a mission and they're my responsibility, and I need to keep myself together.

They walk past me, not saying anything, but not visibly judging either. Besim doesn't push, and we keep walking for another hour. We're nearly at the sighting location. I fall back alongside Besim. There's no time for bad blood or angry words on a mission.

"Sorry," I offer.

He claps me on the shoulder. Silence follows for a few steps when he speaks again.

"You lost your crew, Cieran. We all know how deep that bond goes." His focus sweeps to Dejan and Remy trading low words where they walk ahead of us. "But we all knew someone, had friends, on that mission too. You don't have to carry their memories all by yourself."

Now he's going to get me crying. I swallow hard. Maybe not their memories. But I don't have anyone to share my sister with. Shay's funeral had been me, some of her coworkers, some friends I didn't really know, Dave and Mary Sheridan, and our old caseworker. My crew would have been there with me if I hadn't been at their funerals or memorials already.

A "Yeah," is all I've got. Even that scrapes raw.

He taps my shoulder again and moves off, the offer still silently there.

I'm back up front again when we reach the sighting location. I check the compass and markings just to make sure.

"All right, Rem, do your thing," I say. He's one of the best trackers we have—even without using magic—so he should be able to pick up something to get us on their trail.

But he's locked on to something across the hills. "Don't have to, Sarge. They're coming right at us."

That was the last thing I expected.

"What?" I jog to his side. Remy's not tensed for combat.

Four figures walk in loose diamond formation toward us. The one in front makes our position, and lifts his hands wide.

All the same, I give the order for weapons on standby. Like I said before, dragonwalkers don't usually travel outside the Kirnae Archipelago. They've managed to keep out of the two world wars that came from the Roman Empire falling a hundred and eighty years ago. Some like to say that the Kirnae Islands are remnants of the lost Atlantean islands, but I don't really care about that. All I care about are the four dragonwalkers who've decided to stroll the American Wastelands.

We fall into our own formation, Besim backing me up as I step out in front.

They get closer and the lead lifts his right hand up in the universal sign for peace. I mimic the action, but no one relaxes as they get closer.

All four wear dark, fitted trousers and calf-high boots, along with sleek black undershirts and forearm braces. On top are old-style breastplates with a faint sheen to them. The harness on the breastplate looks modern, like someone had upgraded them and kept just the design old-school.

It looks pretty sweet.

Then there are the short swords, knives strapped to legs or belts, light packs. The dragonwalkers look like they can move and leave us in the dust. And this is just in human form. *If* they actually are dragon shifters and the grif squad wasn't high on something.

"Well met," the man says. He and his team all have deep brown skin tinged with a bit of copper. Now that we're face-to-face, there's a sharpness to his eyes, something about the way he stands that makes me think he might actually be a shifter. Like he's tensed for sudden action.

I arch an eyebrow at the old-school greeting. "Hi."

"I am Dimos Kostas, captain in the dragonfleet."

Definitely sounds like common is not his first language. But at least he can speak it, since the three languages I know don't include dragonwalker.

"Cieran O'Donnell. Sergeant." I extend my hand. He clasps it.

"You are Drax Guard?"

"And you're a dragonwalker?" I shift my stance a little. Technically, the Guard got its start fighting wingless fire drakes, but we've been known to tussle with dragons in the last two hundred years before they all went to ground.

He chuckles, teeth flashing white and a little eerily pointed against his darkened skin. The sunlight catches that same coppery glint to his short hair.

"Yes. We didn't think we would find anyone else out here, but we caught your scent a few hours ago."

The Wastelands tend to leave you with a sort of singed aroma. My nose is already numbed to it, but I'm not a shifter with an enhanced sense of smell.

"What are the four of you doing out here?"

"Last I knew, this land was not under anyone's jurisdiction." Contention layers Dimos's voice.

"And last we knew, dragonwalkers haven't shown their faces this side of the Atlantica in over ninety years." I try to keep my tone even. "So you'll excuse us for coming to check it out in Allied States' territory."

He flashes the smile with the hint of sharpness again. "You have a point."

"And?" I prompt. I used to be a lot more tactful about these sorts of things, I promise.

"We are chasing a human sorcerer. We believe him to have come from your western territories fourteen months ago. He has been wreaking havoc on some of our islands and the Lusitanian coastal cities, trying to form some sort of caster organization and steal dragonwalker secrets." Dimos's eyes narrow. "We came close to catching him, but he escaped weeks ago. We have tracked him here."

Dread starts to pool in my gut. I've never prayed very much—that was Shay's thing—but I'm about to if it'll stop him naming who I think he's going to.

"He goes by Andrej."

My heart almost stops and the ashy earth is about to give way underneath me. I can only stare at him as shocked murmurs come from my crew.

"He's dead." The words come out all strangled and pleading. He has to be dead.

Dimos's gaze pierces through me. "You know him?"

Some sort of noise erupts from me. "He took out almost an entire crew out here fourteen months ago, and I...he's *dead*."

But I hadn't been fully conscious for the end of it. The grif squad and crew who'd flown out after we missed a key check-in had found bodies. At least I'd had that to hold on to. Andrej was dead and wouldn't kill another crew or set off another bomb of wild magic in a city square, or unleash monsters on the innocent.

Dimos's hand stretches between us—pacifying or ready to brace me up. "I am sorry, but he is very much alive."

"Cieran?" Besim nudges my shoulder. I lift my wild gaze to him and see the rest of the crew gathering around. They know the name, but maybe not so well as I do.

My crew had tracked the sorcerer for months before finally pinning him down in the Wastelands.

Dimos's reply breaks through my shock. "All we want is to bring him to justice. He has many crimes to answer for, and it seems many in your states as well. I have been authorized to make whatever alliances we need to bring him in." He extends his hand again.

I can think of nothing but a bright light and searing pain and loss. Still, a part of me mechanically reaches toward him. Our palms collide in agreement.

"Our camp is not far from here," Dimos says. I nod and give the order to fall in.

As I do, I glance at the other dragonwalkers. Something about the fourth catches me off guard. One look into dark eyes shot with gold, and an invisible hit slams into my chest so hard I take a step back.

My hand presses against the armored vest, expecting to find some sort of weapon or magic blast burrowing towards my heart. Nothing. I look up again, taking in a few more details. A woman, compact build, coppery tinted hair wrapped around her head in a braid. And a face scowling at me in mutual disbelief and shock.

You've got to be kidding me.

5

Cieran

The dragonwalker reaches the conclusion the same time I do. It's all over her slim face. She takes a step back and I almost do the same trying to move away from the invisible tether reaching between us. I slam up a mental wall like I might against mind-readers and the sharp sensation fades. But I'm still off-balance.

"Athina?" Dimos swivels toward her.

She shakes her head and says something in a fluid language. All the while glaring at me as if I had anything to do with it.

"Cieran?" The others gather around me. I'm still staring like an idiot.

Dimos lurches forward and grabs my vest, hauling me close. That snaps instincts into place. I have a knife at his throat before either of us blink.

"What are you trying?" he snarls, all trace of friendship gone. A hint of fire stirs the air between us.

"I could ask you the same thing," I reply. This is the absolute last thing I need out here.

His eyes narrow, and there's a deepening to the copper color. He's not even phased by the knife's edge pressing to his skin. "You felt it too?"

"Yeah, and I'm just as thrilled as she is, believe me."

"Sergeant?" Besim pushes for answers.

Dimos scoffs and pushes me away. Everyone's got weapons pulled. I spread my hands and carefully sheathe the knife. My crew backs up a step and cautiously lower weapons. The silver sheen to Besim's skin fades, the stoneskin from his dad's side and a better protection than most armor. Remy closes his hand, extinguishing the hint of deep blue magic he'd pulled.

Dimos gives a thin smile, and the dragonwalkers also disengage. They sheathe weapons and the tallest shifter steps away from the woman like he's no longer about to shield her from me. Dark green scales fade from the third soldier's cheeks.

"What's going on?" Remy asks this time, voice low.

I shake my head, hating that I have to put it into words. "Looks like she and I have a heartbond." Just mentioning it makes the bond pulse against the mind block, almost busting free with how it feels. Both strange and familiar.

Dejan barks a laugh and stabs his arrow back into the quiver.

"Not funny, Dej," I grumble.

"If you think about how many variables of chance aligned, yes, it is."

I take it back. Maybe I don't like him.

Remy rubs the back of his neck. "You can't really mess around with those, right?"

"There's no good way to get rid of it. Especially if you both choose it." Dejan's mouth flattens as he holsters his bow and hooks thumbs around his vest straps.

I don't know all the fine details, but it doesn't matter because I'm not choosing her and she's not choosing me and we're not getting stuck together for life.

"This is not what we're here to discuss. We've got a criminal to track, and this time he's staying dead."

"Or we're taking him alive," Besim interjects, a slight rise to his eyebrow.

"Yeah." I yank one of my pack straps. *Or*, his body is getting left for the scavengers.

Dimos doesn't let up his glare as I stalk forward a step. His crew doesn't move for weapons again. The dragonwalker woman, Athina, looks just as frigid.

"This is not changing anything," I state. "Our crews will work together to take down Andrej, and then we go our separate ways."

"Who gets Andrej?" he asks.

"As long as he gets taken care of and is locked up, or more preferably dead, I don't really *firren* care."

Dimos studies me a moment, then gives a sharp nod. We head out in our separate groups, the dragonwalkers leading the way. She gives me one more look before setting her sights straight ahead. I have no idea if she speaks common.

Maybe that'll make the next few days easier. Afterwards we'll split, put miles between us, and wait for the bond to wither out and die.

6

Athina

A human?

I'd be offended if this new sensation wasn't pulsing so brightly in my chest. It is like a merry flame bringing added warmth to my internal fire. Destiny is a wild and chaotic force at times, but in others she is sure and steady like a river wearing down the roots of a mountain. As the elf said, the number of variables that would have to align to bring us together here is high.

Dragonwalkers stay close to our islands, but the dragonfleet has regular interactions with the Lusitanian and African coastal cities. The few humans, elves, or fae who live on Kirnae have been there for generations and can be trusted. But nothing like this has been reported in hundreds, if not more, years. Heartbonds are not common in any of the species. Cross-species bonds are even more rare. We dragonwalkers have not had one outside our own people in generations.

At least the human sergeant is just as displeased as I am. This will make it easier in the long run. I've seen couples right after the bond activated and they can hardly keep their hands off each other. But mostly that had been other dragonwalkers, and we are a more passionate group if the reports are to be believed.

After all, it was a dragon who sought out a sea witch to turn him into a human to explore for a time, and then fell in love with a human woman along the way. Their child was the first dragonwalker. The fire of that ancient dragon still burns in our hearts.

Silence lingers between our two fleets. Or crew. Whatever it is he said they were called.

Not quite. Some murmurs come from them. They all seem concerned about him from the way questions are tossed about and he glares back. Him. Cieran.

"Athina?" Christakis Lagana leans a little closer. He has the darkest skin of all of us, the brightest eyes, and even the military cut can't contain his curled hair. Small throwing knives strapped to his forearms and the sides of his boots wait to be used with deadly accuracy.

"I'm fine." I don't mean to snap, but I'm off-balance like I've caught a surprise updraft under my wings.

He hums, a low frequency that reaches out to try to soothe me. He's been a fleetmate for three years, as tough a fighter on two legs as he is in his dark-scaled form.

"The mission comes first." It always does. "It seems he thinks the same."

The hum comes again. "What if the bond gets in the way?"

"What, you think I'll throw myself at him?" I scoff, offended he thinks so poorly of me.

This time he chuckles. "I am thinking more of him. We don't seek out other countries as much as Americans, or humans, do."

"So I'm some exotic feature? That's disgusting."

He huffs in exasperation.

"That's exactly what it sounded like, Takis."

He allows it with a shrug. "It's not completely what I meant."

Dimos turns his attention now. "Keep your head on, Athina."

His words are sparse, neatly packed like his clothes and kit. Efficient. Like me, he comes from a long line of warriors, and can trace his lineage back to the first dragon. In his dragon form he can outfly us all. Long ago, a copper stay was placed along his ribs to dampen some of the shifter power from completely overwhelming his human form.

I give him a pitying look. "So little faith from my fleetmates."

Iosef glances my direction. "Introduce yourself at least. It will make working together less awkward, and place the bond at ease."

He has a bond with his wife, so he knows the pull. Iosef Buros is the oldest in our fleet by a few years, has more years of service on his record, and infinitely more patience than Takis. As such, he can be the listening ear for all of us, even Dimos. I give him a little nod and get one of his frequent smiles back.

"Is there a way to get rid of this?"

All three shrug. Unhelpful males. They probably wouldn't care if it was a female walking opposite with a bond in place with them. But I do know that as long as we don't accept the bond, it will remain a surface level attraction and connection trying to draw us to the other.

I risk a glance over. *Cieran* has his face set forward, a tenseness in his jaw. There's a slight bobble in his step, the way his right foot places on the ground. The wind merrily skips past him, giving me a nose full of his scent.

These Wastelands *stink*, and it's covered him, but there is also a hint of metal about him, more than his weapons. He'd seemed shocked to hear about Andrej, saying the bastard had killed soldiers out here not long ago. Was he part of that fleet?

We get to our camp and there is some shuffling to rearrange our packs and give them some room. They set up on the far end, a space between our fleets.

For a moment we all stare at each other. I mostly try to avoid Cieran. But he stirs first, dragging my attention to him anyway.

"What do you have so far?" he asks.

Dimos pulls out his tablet from his trouser pocket. It seems to be momentarily working since he doesn't put it away immediately. Cieran has a notebook and map tucked together. They stand closer together as Dimos gives the results of two days' scouting out here.

In short, nothing.

Cieran rubs the side of his jaw. "Okay. I know this area pretty well, even if it's been a bit since I've been out." There's a hesitation over those words. "But nothing really changes out here."

He flips to a clean page of the notebook and tucks a pencil behind his ear. The map unfolds by two squares.

"Here we are." The pencil comes back to tap the map. "About ten miles that way"—he jabs the pencil to the west—"there's a small settlement. Some vagrants have holed up there. He didn't head there last time. I doubt he would again."

He sounds so certain. The pencil tucks between his teeth as he rearranges the map again. The bond jolts annoyingly like it's actually attached to my heart. I have no idea how this infuriating thing works, so I'm hoping he doesn't notice my heart jumping like a dragonwalker seeing her crush shift for the first time.

"Here's where we tracked him to months ago." The pencil is gone, and he's back to pointing at the map.

Dimos narrows his eyes. "That is thirty miles south."

We share some of Dimos's frustrated disbelief. It's the wrong direction from where we've been searching for days.

"Yeah." A humorless smile tilts Cieran's mouth. "We got lucky last time. Got a tracking charm on one of his guys. Followed it a fair ways out here before they found it, but we were hot on the trail by then. There's some ruins he set up in. He had a stash of weapons, supplies, and magic in there. Doubt he detonated it all on us." A bleak smile spreads.

"Do you think he'll head there again?" Dimos crosses his arms.

He shrugs. "It's where I'd head if I knew I had a weapons cache out here. How many guys he have this time?"

"Between ten and twenty. We never got a good count." The admission is hard for Dimos. He likes exact numbers and facts.

The sergeant nods. "Sounds about right. He doesn't like sharing, but he'll have enough to do some of the dirty work for him."

Cieran folds up the map, then scrawls some notes on the paper. "We were given four days to get out here and scout. Make contact if possible. We'll send a message back to our CO and let him know what's going on. I don't know anything about dragonwalkers except what the stories say, but he took out most of a Drax crew last time. We might need some more backup."

Dimos stands a little taller. If he were in dragon form, his wings would be up and his head pulled back in challenge. "Do what you think you must."

The rest of us stir. We are the best fleet for the job and if we can't do it, it will be hard to show our wings for awhile.

Cieran angles a look at Dimos, weighing. Then he gives a little shrug. "Okay. Besim, get it started and send it off. We've still got some daylight. Want to cover some more miles before then?" He tucks away the map.

The man who has the mild, earthy scent of troll about him heads to his pack and kneels, pulling out a tablet. He taps at it for a moment before shaking his head at the sergeant. Likely the same issue we've been having with electronics. Something about this place keeps them flickering on and off. Besim fishes out some paper and a slender cylinder instead.

He towers above the others, looming over Takis, our tallest member, by at least two more inches. At least the two humans seem average beside him. The shorter elf looks comically small in comparison. I study the human who is not Cieran. There's the hint of fire about him and an echo of something calling to the dragon inside.

I have never been to the Pacifica Island nation of Hawaii. However, I'm willing to wager he has their ancestry and carries the flames of a magma dragon.

We pack up the small bits we'd left out that morning. The Drax crew stands by easily, waiting. Besim works on the message. My pack is in place, and this bond, annoying.

Cieran stands slightly off to the side, tapping his sunglasses against his hand as he waits for his soldier. Huffing exasperation, I stride forward. Iosef said an introduction would place this hopping bond at ease. I want to stop feeling unsteady inside and to see what kind of man fate thinks it can bind me to.

He looks up in surprise that turns to wariness as I stop in front of him.

"Athina Spera." I stick out my hand.

If anything, he gets a little more tense. "Cieran O'Donnell." But his returning handshake is firm.

My muscles jitter like I need to shift and take flight. But I stay ground-ed. His crew is watching, leaning a little closer. I don't need to turn around to see the stares my fleet are giving me. I incline my head in question, and we step away for some bare semblance of privacy.

Once there, we just sort of stare at each other. Now that I'm fully face-to-face with him, and not looking just off to the side, or at the patches or bits of his armor, I am a little unhappy that I like what I see.

We're the same six feet tall. Dark hair is crammed under the hat he clearly doesn't understand how to wear. The strands are longer than a normal severe military cut, but the rest of his crew wears their hair the same way. His hazel eyes are surrounded by lines from squinting in the sun, maybe some laugh lines, but the way his mouth is pressed together, it doesn't look like he's laughed in awhile. Tanned skin, and a familiarity with the way he wears his weapons. He's been at this for a few years, but he looks around my age of twenty-seven. I know that dragonwalkers and humans at least age at the same rate.

But physical appearance doesn't matter if he shows himself to be dishonorable.

"Hey." He breaks the awkwardness first. "I'm not looking...or expecting anything." Caution lines up his shoulders.

"I'm not either," I reassure. I had to fight fist and claw to be where I am, for this place in the fleet. And this bond? This feels like it is undermining me, cutting wing tendons to send me falling.

"Okay."

I think he tries to hide how relieved he is. It calms me in a way, even though the bond is snarling around my heart, impatient with me.

"So we're good to finish out this mission and then part ways?" he asks.

"I have no problem with that." But I pause. "I'm not sure what happens to...this." My hand flicks between us.

"Yeah." He rubs his jaw again. "There's some stories that say time and distance can sort of kill it off. As long as..."

As long as neither of us change our minds before we part ways and choose to cement the bond firmly in place. Which won't happen.

"The distance should be no problem." I give a faint smile. The Kirnae Islands are leagues away and most are accessible only to dragonwalkers.

"Cir!" Besim calls him.

The shortened form of his name almost suits him better.

"Okay, well...nice to meet you, Athina." He nods and heads over to the other soldier.

Iosef waits as I step back over to them, poised with one of his deeply searching questions, but Dimos pushes his way forward.

"Don't worry." I give him a glare that sends him backing off slightly. "We're keeping our interactions professional."

Dimos grunts and heads off. Iosef just gives me a look that's a little sad, but nods, and leaves me alone. I catch his hand brushing the copper inlaid bond dampening bracelet he wears on missions to protect his wife. Their heartbond is fully accepted and if something happened to him, she would feel it. Another reason I don't want this.

My gaze strays back to the American fleet, to Cieran. He did not question why I was here, how I have a place in the fleet. He treated me as an equal, and that makes me look a little kinder toward him.

Besim stands and does something to the cylinder to make it sprout wings and take off from his hands. The device speeds into the sky and away from the Wastelands. Cieran tracks its path a moment and I catch desperation in the tilt of his head, like he wishes he could be following it out. Then he tucks the glasses on, obscuring the hazel eyes which had held a multitude of things, and he and Dimos take lead out.

I make sure to stay at the back of the fleet. This is going to be a long few days.

7

Cieran

I really wish she hadn't come over to introduce herself. Now I've got a full name and a stupid heartbond doing jumping jacks in my chest. Or maybe that's just the exhaustion from only getting two hours of sleep last night. The mental block isn't doing much to keep the bond out anymore, so I ease up on it.

Athina wears her armor and weapons like they're a part of her. A bit of the copper in her eyes tinges the brown hair she's got braided around the side of her head and tucked up at the back. She looks like she can kick ass and not break a sweat.

It was fine until she came over, because now I've got a new awareness of her like something's threaded between us and about to pull. That thread means I know she's at the back of this crew.

At least we're on the same page. But every time I think it's fine, that this is just one more thing I need to suppress to get through the next few days, my heart does a swan dive right into my gut and laughs all the way back up to pummel my chest.

Remy and I take point. After another five-mile walk with the sunset glaring all the way down beyond the horizon, we find a new campsite. We set up and figure out a watch order with our new friends.

I think everyone knows what we're trying to do, because Athina and I are not paired up. In fact, we're on opposite watches, so we shouldn't have to run into each other.

Dinner passes quietly, with some attempts at conversation between crews. I don't join in. The only thing bigger than a heartbond is hearing that Andrej is alive and still up to his old mayhem. Some garbage about equality without restrictions and the established laws on magic and caster levels. Like he's not an air warlock turned sorcerer by stealing magic from others or siphoning it from the natural deposits the world over. It's just an excuse to throw around his stolen magic and illegal spells and power-trip on hurting helpless people and weaker magic users.

I saw plenty of that "equality" in bombed buildings, injured civilians, and burned-out magic preserves. We were one step behind him for months until I pulled in Ylan to infiltrate. He got a tracker on one of Andrej's minions and we caught up.

Andrej is still alive, and my team died for nothing.

It brings the cloud-covered sky pressing a little closer on top of me and churns the dust kicked up by our boots a little thicker as it clogs my throat.

I'm on second watch, but there's no way I'm falling asleep now. I head to the edge of camp where some rocks perch and start cleaning and checking weapons.

Besim's heavier steps come over. I grit my teeth and keep burnishing my broadsword.

"How you doing, Sarge?" A slight exhale accompanies him sitting beside me.

"Thinking I'm going to ban that question for the next three days."

A rough chuckle shakes Besim's chest. He pulls out his own equipment and goes to work on his longsword.

Another inhale comes from Besim but I cut him off. "I don't want to talk about anything right now."

"Figured. I was going to ask if I could borrow a smaller knife. The lid on this stupid thing won't come off."

The lid of his leather oil isn't budging, even for him. And him using one of his two dirks to get it off is begging for an injury. I give him my smallest knife and he pries open the container.

As he hands it back, I ask, "Why are you here?"

There's plenty of spots by the small smokeless fire where he can clean equipment.

He shrugs. "Didn't want you to feel alone."

I wipe the cloth down the length of the blade, blinking furiously. True to his word, he doesn't say anything, and packs up as I finish. My sword feels heavy in my hand as I stand, like it doesn't really want to be out here either.

"Thanks," I finally say.

Besim nods. "You're part of Crew Six for the mission, Cir. You're not alone."

A multitude of things snarl up in my throat. I shift the broadsword so the sheathed edge isn't digging so hard into my palm.

"Sort of got used to feeling that way." The admission keeps me a little off-balance.

He nods. "We're glad to have you around. Even if Dejan doesn't say anything."

It gets me to crack a smile. "Marcel was like that." My voice twists a little at the end and I sniff.

Besim chuckles. "Yeah, I remember that about him."

But the forefront of my memories is the half-fae, shorter than average and all-scowls to people he didn't know, lying twisted, armor smoking and dusky blue eyes ringed in vibrant fae grey staring sightlessly back at me through a mess of blood.

I scrub the heel of my hand under my eye and sniff again. "Fates, I don't know if I'm going to make it through this."

Besim's hand clamps down on my shoulder, not saying anything as I manage to get it under control with another sharp breath.

"Hearing Andrej's name caught us all by surprise. Like I said, you're not out here alone. We'll get him this time. For them." Determination radiates off him.

He releases me as I rock back. "Sorry you guys got stuck with me. I don't think I should be out here. Probably should have just taken the discharge months ago." I laugh bitterly.

"Felt like giving up?"

I nod, but it's more than that. The Drax Guard has been my family for six years, and the military for ten. Shay's the other reason for me enlisting and being here today—we'd talked it out on the Sheridans' kitchen floor late at night two days after I'd turned eighteen, sharing fruit loops right from the box. The too-vivid memory stings again.

"We're not sorry you're out here with us. I know all of us are glad you're trying to find your feet again. None of us like seeing a Drax brother grounded."

I'm not the first one. Won't be the last one. Even my old crew had lost a brother to an injury he couldn't shake. But he still met up with us until his family moved cities.

We head back to the fire. I go to my bedroll, crouching as I dig through my pack for the pain pills I still need every now and then. All this walking has left my leg above the prosthetic sore in a way it hasn't been since the most intense days of therapy. The meds go down with a bare swig of water. I take a deep breath and scrape a hand through my hair, dislodging some dust. Standing, I belt my sword on and check knives and the straps of my vest before heading out for my watch.

A tugging at my chest has me looking up across the fire. The light glints off a pair of dark eyes ringed in copper. Nothing in Athina's face betrays her, but she sees me looking back and lies down, turning away from me.

Well, the feeling's mutual. I pull my hat on, and head out.

———

Athina's watching me again over breakfast. It makes my bar taste even drier and the heartbond restart its incessant tugging trying to get me to return the look. Also makes me think she noticed me awake when she left and came back from her watch. I'd already gotten my three hours of sleep for the night by then. My body has gotten used to it after fourteen months. If we weren't out on a mission, I'd crash later in the afternoon for a few hours, and start the cycle over again.

My therapist and I haven't successfully gotten my sleep schedule figured out. But honestly there are a lot bigger things going on in my head he's been trying to get through.

Dimos comes over, wanting to set a precise schedule for the day—how many miles we're walking, how many stops, when I think we'll be close enough to send out scouts. It's making my headache worse.

The heartbond sort of settles as I refuse to look at Athina. It's keeping an off-beat to my heartrate, cheerily reminding me that it's there and I haven't done anything about it. Which also isn't helping my head.

I rub a thumb across my temple and try to stay patient with Dimos. Pissing off a dragonwalker probably isn't a good way to start a day. Plans are eventually set without breaking any alliances.

We get packed up and fall into the same walking and scouting pattern as before. She's closer this time. Guess everyone trusts us not to fall over each other.

Two hours trudging and we hit a wide-open space that stretches in all directions. It's too flat, like something tamped it down and erased any vegetation or natural ridge. I scrape a hand over my forehead, dislodging my cap slightly. Open spaces like this aren't good in the Wastelands.

"Eyes out," I say quietly. There's no way around it, and a quick glance at the map confirms that it stretches out for a good three miles in all directions.

The dragonwalkers look over the landscape with the same alertness as us, but Dimos angles his attention to me.

I answer the unspoken question. "The wars that created this place were hundreds of years ago, but there's still some nasty stuff you can trigger. And there's usually some critters out and about on the plains. They're fast on even ground, so they'll outrun you, no matter how quick you are. We'll be lucky to get across this without seeing anything."

Remy crouches and places fingertips against the soil. We wait in silence until he looks to me. His dark brown eyes squint against the glaring sunlight, the surrounding lines not deepened by concern or warning. Yet.

"Clear for now." He rises to his feet and gives a humorless smile. "Just step light."

Another unspoken rule of the Guard besides "trust Besim's advice" is "trust Remy's magic."

"Careful of shifting until we're across," Remy tells the dragonwalkers. "That's a different kind of magic that might still trigger something."

Dimos inclines his head. "We've already encountered that."

The tall dragonwalker, Takis, moves, his shoulders twitching restlessly. He's probably the one who learned that the hard way.

Even if they do shift, the rest of us are on foot. The grif squads are the exceptions to the "it's bad manners to ask a flying shifter for a ride." I'm not gambling that these shifters will carry us. Things can change in an instant out here, no matter how prepped you are, or what checks you run. As for other options, Remy's strength doesn't lie in making gates, and even if it did, magic that size would draw everything on these plains to us and put us in an even worse spot. We're better off just walking.

Dejan sets an arrow on his bow, and we all check weapons. Swearing softly, I step out. My crew spreads out in a line. We know how to traverse this. The dragonwalkers wait a few beats before following our lead. We move slow and cautious, pausing every hundred feet or so for Remy to keep checking. Our boots whisper forward until Remy pulls to an abrupt halt.

We do the same. I'm all but holding my breath as I listen.

There's a pop like an air-bubble bursting underwater. A small hole opens ten paces away. Grains of dirt slide into it, tumbling faster and faster like they want to smother the thing inside. And the clicking starts.

Remy draws the basalt sword on his back with a resigned curse.

"Let's move!" I pull my sword and we all sprint forward.

Dimos catches up with me. "I thought you said we can't outrun whatever it is?"

I check over my shoulder. The ground is undulating and bursting. "Better to get a head start. You have any fire handy?"

He grins and his teeth seem to sharpen a little.

Dejan whips around, still running backwards, and looses an arrow. A gurgling shriek answers.

One down. Probably way too many to go.

"Incoming!" Besim warns.

"Fall in."

We slide to a stop, settling into a three-man shield around Remy who's summoning dark blue fire from his hands. I risk a glance over the dragonwalkers. They've spread out in a line, weapons drawn.

This doesn't deter the mentarin. They're about three feet tall, with ten legs and plenty of stabbing appendages. Mouths full of razor-sharp teeth that'll rip prey to shreds in seconds once they get ahold of it. And they hunt in packs.

We've got thirty at least bearing down on us. There's no reasoning with these things. History has mentarin first appearing in the civil wars centuries ago, some sort of twisted creation by one side. The remnants that survived the volcanic fallout adapted and reproduced in their tunnels under the Wastelands, with a few mutations thrown in like the other surviving creatures out here.

This place *firren* sucks.

I tap the band on my left wrist and the shield springs out. Dejan's bow is singing. He takes out another two before they launch themselves at us. He slams his bow into the quiver's holster and gets to work with his sword. The first mentarin latches on to my shield. I stab around the rim, and it falls. I barely feel the reverberations as another collides with the surface. The dwarves did an awesome job on the upgrades.

"Clear!" Remy shouts.

Besim and I sidestep, giving him a path to blast a ray of fire that heats the side of my face and leaves a bit of hair singed.

Mentarin shriek and scatter, but they're hungry, so they keep coming. Sticky green blood coats my sword, but the rhythm of swings and stabs is almost hypnotic. They don't have much in the way of tactics, being pretty single-minded, so it's just a matter of staying in front of the pack.

Hack and slash, step aside for another blast from Remy. Repeat.

A deeper roar of fire and brighter heat flashes on my left side. I jerk my shield up to protect that side automatically before I realize it's a dragonwalker. Dimos is still human but fire wicks around his mouth and crackles along his sword hand.

The mentarin come to an uncertain halt.

Until another series of pops and clicks sounds. We've woken another pack. One that hasn't learned some slight caution of dragon fire. Remy draws his other sword.

"Back up," I say, shifting my grip on the shield.

Dimos and his crew mimic us as the next pack of mentarin surface and start coming for us. Some stop and start gorging on the corpses of their dead brethren. No respect out here either.

Maybe this pack is bigger, or we woke up more than one den. Either way, we've got our hands full as we keep a steady retreat.

A jolt through my chest has my head whipping to the left again. Athina rocks back on her heels, a mentarin impaled on her sword. She shakes it free and scowls through bits of green blood. Her free hand twists and flame appears in her palm. She shoves her hand towards the incoming beasts. Fire erupts, the same wild, ferocious heat that overshadows what Remy can summon.

My attention is pulled away by a guttural roar. Mentarin stop in their tracks, then redouble in intensity as if desperate to get a taste in before our next problem occurs. And it's a big one.

"Cover!"

My shout brings Besim closer to me as I scan the skies. I don't see the beast until it's too late. Dark grey scales evolved to camouflage against the perpetually gloomy sky hid it just long enough.

It's diving and I already know the target. They always go for magic, inhaling it from a user like a drug addict.

It's coming like an arrow.

"Remy, *DOWN*!"

He's got a mentarin on his sword and another one trying to latch on to his arm. Dejan yells something, but I'm already sprinting. Panic lights up Remy's face. The shriek of wind builds against its scales.

I slam a shoulder into him, throwing him to the ground. It puts him right in the path of the mentarin, but he'll stand a better chance with them than with the crendrake.

He hits the ground as claws hook around me. My feet lift off the ground. I'm hurled forward and slammed into the dust. It's on top of me and all I can see is grey.

Dust billows and wind gathers. It's taking off, talons still curled around me.

Shit.

8

ATHINA

MY HEART JOLTS HARD. I hear his cry and then nothing but panic. Some winged, snakelike creature with twisted spikes along its back snatches him up in its claws and takes to the skies.

His fleet are shouting. The warlock tries to get up from the ground. The little creatures are still coming.

And Cieran is disappearing into the sky.

Dimos starts to shout a warning, but I'm already moving, sheathing sword and dumping my pack as I start to shift. Shedding my human form and embracing the dragon. Risking triggering a magic trap like happened two days ago to Takis. My heavy forelegs slam down on the ground. Heat builds in my chest and throat. The savage things stop and I loose a proper fire, incinerating large swaths of them before my wings pump and I launch into the air.

I stretch my long neck as my wings propel me up, up, up, then level out. The heartbond points me right to them, racing across the sky. I dart a little higher, then dive after them. The ground races below us as I gain.

Cieran struggles in the beast's hold, but there's no good angle for him to strike. Even if he did, the resulting fall will kill him unless I somehow catch him first.

The creature starts to dive, plummeting to the ground. My heartrate spikes and panic wells bitter on my tongue. It's Cieran's panic.

This new foe is smaller than me, its dive quicker. It skims low into a wide trench.

Its wings beat, slowing enough to let him fall a few feet to the ground and tumble over and over. It lands and opens a toothless mouth. Cieran just lies there, but a sudden weakness compresses my body and I falter. I'm close now, pulling out of my own dive to see him feebly moving.

Then I open my wings, flipping all four limbs to face the thing, claws extended, and slam into it.

It dies on impact, neck snapping to the side. I didn't even need to use teeth. But I sink talons into its heart to make sure. A savage growl rumbles in my chest, and a small bit of my mind reels in surprise at the intensity of it.

But the heartbond thumps in satisfaction that I protected Cieran.

I turn as he staggers to his feet, sword in front of him. His legs barely hold him. Raw panic shines in his face as his shield wobbles.

It smarts to know I am causing him such distress. Shaking my head, I change back. Take one step forward, wings compressing and scales retreating, to leave me standing on two legs, and clothed with armor and weapons. A few strands of hair are annoyingly out of place.

A shuddering gasp breaks from Cieran. The relief crashes over me, dousing the last of my fire. His sword falls from his hand, and he hits his knees. I sprint forward, but he's still moving. Tapping the inside of his wrist. The shield whirls and disappears.

I sink to a knee beside him. His forearms press to the ground, his head between them. Each breath shakes around a dozen curses.

I dare to reach out and touch his fist. "Are you all right?"

One more breath and then he moves, sitting back on his heels. Dirt and green blood smears across his face, but that hat is still in place despite the fight and the surprise trip he took midair. He just stares at me, and he seems paler than is normal.

"Cieran?" I press.

It makes him jolt. He looks down at himself, patting and taking stock.

"Yeah. Nothing's broken."

His hand closes over his sword, and he pushes up with shaking arms. He staggers once upright, and my hand on his arm keeps him from falling. One, two tries before the weapon is sheathed.

"Thanks." Cieran nods.

I step back with a little reluctance. It means something that I so quickly disregarded our caution of shifting out in these Wastelands. Even though I don't want to be bonded to him, to anyone, I could not abandon him.

"What is that?" I tilt my head back to the creature.

"Crendrake." He starts to walk away from it, each step unsteady. "They go after magic users and drain the magic until the person dies."

Two quick strides bring me to his side. He looks up at the embankments surrounding us, searching for a way out. He stumbles, foot catching on nothing.

"Cieran?" I catch him. "Did it do that to you?"

"No." His smile is forced. "I don't have magic."

I swing around to block his path, placing my hands on his shoulders. "It did something to you." I narrow my eyes, studying him. But I don't know enough about him yet.

He blinks and looks away from my eyes. "Not sure."

Now that I'm touching him, I can feel what's off. Even through several layers of clothes, he's chilled. I hesitantly press a hand against his forehead, confirming it.

"You're cold. It must have drained you of some energy anyway."

A pained sort of smile spreads. "Now that you mention it..." Cieran leans harder into my hands. I get an arm around him, keeping him walking while looking for some place to stop.

Thirty paces later, I find it. Rocks jut out from the side of the trench, forming an overhang and a small, enclosed shelter.

"Here." I point.

"What?" He's stumbled ten times at least in as many steps.

"Lie down. I'm giving you some heat."

"Whoa, what?" He tries to pull away, but his teeth are chattering now.

I roll my eyes. "Relax. You're freezing, and I'm part dragon. My internal core temperature is higher than you humans. I can help you stay warm until your body recovers."

His eyes narrow and lips clamp in distrust, but he lowers to the ground, and shrugs off his pack which is a little lopsided from being landed on. Shoving it into the small space first, he scoots farther back.

"Vest off," I say. *I'm* not taking off my armor, but he needs a few less layers.

He obeys.

"Lie down."

He rolls on his left side. Another glance around at the trench before lying down has me satisfied that we'll be safe for a little while at least. I scoot close, pushing his left arm across his chest, sliding mine under his head and my top arm around him.

"No one hears about this," I growl. It doesn't matter that this is needed, I will not get teased about this *and* the heartbond when we get back.

He tucks his free arm over me and hooks his hand into the back strap of my armor. Grimacing a little, I push my knee between his.

"Why you looking at me?" His voice is muffled where his face is tucked against my neck, each breath tickling a little. "You're the one aggressively cuddling me."

"Shut up."

It takes a little scooting and fidgeting before we're both as comfortable as this is going to get. I focus on letting the fire in my chest grow a little hotter. He twitches again, maybe startled at the heat. It's finding my cheeks. This is practical, but it's making the heartbond go a little crazy, trying to get me to pay more attention to him, the glimpses I saw of him fighting.

"If you tell anyone about this…" I warn again.

"Don't worry." Cieran snorts something like a laugh. "I'm not interested in hearing about it either for the next few days."

Quiet lapses between us. His shivering starts to abate and tension leaks from his muscles.

"How are you doing?" I ask quietly.

"Happy to report that things between us are heating up."

I roll my eyes. "Shut up."

The snort comes again. "But really, it's getting quite steamy in here."

It pulls a reluctant smile from me and a happy little jolt from the heartbond. "I see I got stuck with the idiot."

A muffled chuckle sounds. I shake my head slightly.

My hand on his back moves with his deeper breath. "Thanks for coming after me. And for this."

Unintentionally, my arms tuck a little closer around him. "You're welcome."

Quiet falls between us. I keep a steady heat, even though it's starting to draw an unpleasant smell from the ground around us—somewhere between sulfur and *rot*. I'm about to check on Cieran again when I realize his breath is slow and steady against my neck.

I don't think he slept much last night. Or for a lot of nights from the look of him. He's not shivering so much now, but I don't move. It's a foolish thing to stay here for so long, but he's asleep and he needs it. And there's a bit of pride that I got him to relax. So I stay right where I am, and let him rest.

It takes another half hour before I feel the nudge in the back of my mind. Takis making contact. It's just an impression of a question. *Where are you?*

If we were both in dragon form, we could mindspeak to each other, but the bond is weaker in our human form.

I send back the thought. *Safe.* And a mental picture of the trench.

An image of Cieran pops into my head, though I note idly that it's not how I would have seen him. The hair color is too light and it's not the way he stands.

Safe. I send again. And then an image of the creature, dead by my claws. A bit of satisfaction tinges the bond and I smile grimly. I think of Cieran's fleet. He'll want to know about them when he wakes.

The impression of them all safe comes back.

Another question nudges. It takes some doing to imagine Cieran just lying here asleep without me all wrapped around him. I do not want that one going to my fleetmate.

There's no teasing or pretend shock returning, so I think I'm successful. I get a visual of a map and a location where they're heading. Once Cieran wakes, I'll pass it to him.

He still sleeps soundly. I pull back my heat. He's stopped shivering, but now feels too hot. The heartbond pulses warm in my chest, content next to my heartfire. In fact, it's making me sleepy and content. I fight the urge to curl closer to him and just nap like I'm in dragon form on the black rocks of Chern, my home island, on a summer's day.

Instead, I gently work my hand in and out of a fist to keep blood flowing to my arm underneath his head. It's been gradually losing some feeling. The motion doesn't disturb him.

Time slips over the hour mark and toward a second. The ground presses into my hip and shoulder, but the same sort of hazy contentment lingers. I halfheartedly try to shake it, telling myself this is dangerous out here where I need all senses to stay sharp. And the bigger thought looms that Cieran and I agreed to keep our connection contained so we could separate after the mission.

Even if we wanted the bond, we are soldiers from two different countries separated by leagues and oaths. And I will not discount years of training and duty and loyalty for a man I'm not sure yet is my equal.

He jolts suddenly and rolls away. Caution rushes over me. He pushes halfway up on elbows and blinks bleary eyes. I slowly sit up, careful not to startle him, or ram my head against the overhang which doesn't allow much room.

Cieran looks around. "I fell asleep."

"You look like you needed it."

There's a faint lift to his mouth. "Thanks."

I edge back, giving him a little more room and trying to quiet the heartbond, attempting to block it like I might unwanted mindspeak. He rubs his chest, eyes narrowing.

"Your fleet is safe," I say.

He jerks a look at me. "How do you know?"

"Dragonwalkers have low-level telepathy in human form. I was in contact with Christakis while you were asleep."

A sigh of relief gushes from him. Grabbing his vest and pack, he starts to scoot outside. I give him room and soon we both stand up in the open. Him with a little more grumbling.

Cieran glances at the sky, eyes squinting against the glare. "That sucked."

"You had a fairly graceful landing." My mouth tugs up despite my serious tone.

He arches an eyebrow at me, and finally huffs a laugh. It brings a bit of life to his features, but I shouldn't notice that like I do. Shaking his head, he brushes at his hooded shirt, getting some of the caked mud and blood off. His hat comes off next. He drags a hand through the tangled mess of his hair, dislodging more dirt. But he puts it on the functional way.

"So you do know how to wear a hat correctly. I was beginning to wonder." I shouldn't try to tease. It only makes the bond skip around like a child, tugging with playful abandon.

"Okay, is this commentary going to be a thing, or...?" But the faint grin is back. I can't help but return it. He flies easy with my teasing and returns jokes without a blink.

"Dragonwalkers are naturally very honest people." I shrug.

Cieran eyes me again, then scoops up his vest. "Seems awfully convenient, is all I'm saying." He straps it into place and checks the placement of his weapons, his demeanor seeming to sharpen around the edges. Like I caught a glimpse of the real him for a second, and I'm sad to see it go.

Once his pack is in place, he glances up at the sky again and turns a slow circle.

"I wasn't really paying attention while being carted through the air like a piece of meat, so you remember which direction we came in from?"

"I can do better. You have your map?"

It's still in his pocket. Once he hands it over, I find the location Takis sent.

Cieran pulls out a compass. I let him work, though I could tell him which way is north. A dragon's internal compass is never wrong. But there's something fascinating about watching him as he scribbles on a notepad and checks the map again.

"Okay. Looks like we need to head west and a little south." He tucks everything away and I have to shake myself a little to focus on what he's saying. "Sounds like you can make sure we're headed in the right direction?"

I nod, and then add apologetically, "I could fly us, but we're trying to keep a low profile. And I'd rather not accidentally trigger the traps that seem everywhere."

He agrees. "Shifting is noticeable magic." The faint grin tilts his lips again. "And I'm all good on flying for a bit."

I chuckle. "Where are we climbing out?"

We both turn to scan the trench walls. They're about ten feet tall. It shouldn't be difficult if we can find a place with some handholds.

He gestures to the rocky overhang. "This looks as good a place as any."

We each take one side of the rocky outcropping, slipping and clawing our way up to the top. Once we're standing at the summit, Cieran grimaces and reaches to rub his right knee.

"Are you all right?" I get a sensation of discomfort mixed with annoyance.

"Yeah." He shakes his leg out and puts some extra weight on it. "It'll be fine. Let's go."

I don't know him well enough yet to argue, and we set out. The landscape has returned to the same broken hills and gullies, though this one contains more tumbled spires of rocks. I get an uncomfortable impression that this might have once been some sort of town or city or civilized space. The wind had died for now, and I'm grateful to be out of its constant rush for the first time in days. I prefer wind against scales.

"Hey, um...thanks again, for..." He jabs a thumb over his shoulder.

"You're welcome." I don't mention that I might have accidentally made the bond stronger between us. It was not my intent when trying to keep him from collapsing.

Silence falls. I almost squirm under the weight of it.

"Tell me about your fleet." It practically bursts from me.

Cieran's head jerks toward me and I catch a haunted look in his eyes. Tearing his gaze away, he steps up on a tumbled block of granite and hops down. A breath fights from him.

"Besim is half troll and Communications Specialist. You've got to watch him, or he'll get you talking about feelings." The humor seems forced, but I nod.

"That sounds like Iosef. He'd rather serve up ice cream and open conversations than pull out a weapon or shift into his green-scaled form."

"You can't mess around with ice cream." Cieran shrugs, but there's that glimpse of humor again. Sweet tooth then.

"Pie is better."

He half spins to face me, eyes glinting under the brim of his hat. "*Thank you*! You know how far I have to go to get a decent pie back in Dunhare?"

"Come to the islands." I lean closer. "There's a fried pie shop that could stop a war."

We both pause. I did not mean to invite him.

"That sounds awesome," he admits finally.

"What about the others?" I push us back on track.

"Dejan is the resident stoic elf."

"Ah, the other one who doesn't understand the point of a hat."

He frowns at me, but the laugh is there anyway. "He doubles as the crew medic. Elf magic helps out there."

"What about the one that *thing* went after?" I've already forgotten what he called it, but some creatures don't deserve to have their memory kept alive with their name.

"Remy. He's a warlock. Really strong with his innate magic and can control some wild magic, and just as good with his swords. And he can track a moth in a snowstorm."

Our conversation pauses for a moment as we clamber over another rock pile blocking the sort of path we're following through the hills.

"And you?" I ask.

He shrugs. "Just good with a sword."

I think he's selling himself very short. "How long have you been with them?"

I've said something wrong because Cieran freezes, and heartache wraps around me. I definitely made the bond stronger. His emotions are sharper now as they bounce off me.

"Two days." He offers a smile that's painfully forced. "What about you and your crew?"

I accept the subject change. "We've been a fleet for four years now. Dimos has been fleet leader the whole time. He's very precise and methodical."

"I noticed," he says wryly, and I chuckle.

"But he makes good decisions, since they are less ruled by the impulsive dragon side. Takis is stronger than any of us with mindspeak, so he handles communications. Iosef has the brightest fire. He has some other magic as well that he can use, which makes him stronger than the rest of us."

"And you?"

I feel a little awkward talking about myself when he hasn't shared much that is personal. "Stealth flyer, scout, good with a sword." I close the gap between us with a step as I mimic what he said.

Cieran allows it with a faint grin, shifting his hands around his pack straps. "They still doing okay?" His chin angles up, out into the Wastelands in front of us.

Takis responds instantly to my mental question. He sends a picture of both fleets trudging onward to the rendezvous point, looking no more battered than before.

"All good," I reassure and send my own update. The mindspeak is stronger, so we are at least heading in the right direction.

Pebbles shift down the slope to our left. My muscles tense. The acrid scent of the Wastelands tries to obscure any scent, but I still catch a whiff of acid. Cieran scans the path ahead, then looks back over his shoulder.

Slowly, carefully, he crouches to brush a finger over a patch of something light grey on the nearby rock. I grimace as his fingers come back coated in residue. He sniffs the substance. My skills as a scout are faltering out here where our intel only covered a fraction of the dangers and obstacles. But he's clearly familiar with it.

"How do you feel about spiders?" he whispers so softly I might as well just be reading his lips.

"How big?"

The arch of his eyebrow sends my lip curling in disgust. Of course.

I point up to where the rocks have been displaced. He nods and indicates the rise on our other side.

A faint rasp marks him getting his sword ready to draw. Flame builds hotter in my chest, and I reach for my sword.

The spiders attack.

9

Cieran

REGULAR SPIDERS, I DON'T have an issue with. Unless they're the fuzzy ones, which just seem gross. But guess what? Here in the Wastelands, spiders mutated years ago to come in extra-large packages the size of small cars complete with toxic green venom.

Three of them jump over the rise at us. Two at Athina and one at me. I slam a hand on the shield band. It whirls free as I unsheathe my sword.

My back crashes into something solid and there's a comforting rush through the bond. Athina.

I haven't felt this certain going into a fight in fourteen months.

The spider scuttles down the hillside. I whip my shield up to block the jet of acid it spits. It hisses and jumps forward. Shield up again, I make a sweeping strike with my blade and hit a leg. It buckles and I move forward, bracing against a body slam from the spider. But I'm underneath the thing now. It becomes a hacking and slashing game to get through the carapace while dodging more strikes from legs and its twisting attempts to shoot venom or web.

After indeterminable seconds, it backs up, my shield scraping against its underside as it goes, and vanishes over the hill, dragging two injured limbs with it.

A sharp tug through the heartbond has me spinning to Athina. One spider wriggles and hisses at the flames grimly burning through its stomach and side. I move to back her up.

The last spider rears up among steaming acid patches, legs reaching for her.

I whip my shield up and around her, sheltering us both from the acid stream that collides with the surface. Our harsh breath mingles together. Her eyes are bright with fight and fire, and the copper is glowing.

One look and we come to agreement. I charge forward, swiping up with my shield and slamming it back onto its hind limbs. Then I duck as a jet of fire roars overhead, catching the beast in the vulnerable section of mandibles and eyes.

It wails and its legs buckle, bringing it perfectly in range for me to plunge my sword through its mouth and kill it.

Fresh shock pummels through my chest, nearly sending me keeling over. I spin to see Athina slamming to the ground, web wrapped around her legs. The spider that had retreated is back for more, and trying to pull her uphill on a dragline as it backs toward the rise.

Anger sharper than anything I've ever experienced rages through me. I'm moving again. One swing severs the web, and the spider unleashes another sticky attack. It globs onto my shield, and I dig my boots into the ground, resisting its pull.

Athina's on her feet, and an unsettlingly deep growl comes from her. I've never actually heard anyone *growl*. It's pretty terrifying.

"Head down."

I obey her command. Her arm thumps over the shield, her body braced against mine. Fire spews forth from her hand, racing up the web. There's a panicked shriek and smell of burning spider.

Nothing stirs for a few long moments, and then the realization that we are *very* close rushes into my brain. We both lurch away from each other, but I can't help but stare at her. Athina's eyes still blaze, literally, and coppery red scales have burst in diagonal patches down her cheeks. Her stance—sword in one hand and flame dying around her fingers—have got my heart doing kickflips against my ribs.

"I'm done with this place." Her voice still holds a smoky edge, and I'm locked into her gaze. "Are you okay with flying?"

I just stare at her. Athina shakes her head and sheathes her sword. Backing up, she rolls her neck side to side and then her shoulders. Wings sprout from her back, and she's tipping forward. I think belatedly I need to catch her, but scales are sprouting across her face and hands.

Thick, scaly forelimbs thud against the ground. The rest of her fades, transforming faster than my brain can process until she's a fifty-foot-long dragon, two times my height, and covered in coppery red scales.

My mouth hangs open, and I back up to give her more room on the path between the hills and spider carcasses.

In dragon form, her long head still somehow mimics the shape of her angular features. And the eyes are still the same. Dark and flecked in copper, a bit of wildness in them that isn't there when she was human. Or maybe it is. I've been trying to avoid looking directly into her eyes for extended periods.

Athina regards me, waiting.

I'm not really sure what to do with the way I'm feeling right now. Pride that I'm heartbonded to her, a little bit of terror, and an even stronger pull toward her, though part of me is still gamely resisting it.

"That's pretty sweet," I admit. Her neck arches. She's pleased at the reaction, and I grin faintly.

She twists her neck and indicates her back with nose. *Climb on.* The words are loud and clear in my mind, and I stagger back.

"*What* the hell?"

She rears back, a snort of surprise sending a plume of smoke my way.

"*You can hear the mindspeak?*"

Yep, definitely her voice *in my head*. I fold forward, hands on knees, trying to breathe. This got overwhelming fast. Because heartbonds weren't enough, now we've got *firren* telepathy.

"Oh, this is not happening."

The tip of her red snout appears, and tendrils of smoke have me straightening and glaring at her while trying not to cough. But a definite, and very toothy, grin splits her dragon face.

"Yeah, laugh it up." But I'm shaking my head and cleaning my sword on my trousers. Collapsing the shield and sheathing the blade, I roll my neck side to side.

"Can we agree not to do that anymore?" I ask, not really sure where we stand on the whole "let's keep it professional so we can go our separate ways" thing now. The hours I slept next to her, and then this fight have left a stronger pull toward her, but I'm still not taking it any farther than the surface level connection. I don't want—or need—someone new. I need the people who aren't here anymore.

It's a little disconcerting seeing a dragon anyway. To see one nodding has me blinking.

"Okay." I move to her side, switching my cap backwards. A tinge of annoyance sparks as I do. It has to be from Athina, and I give her a smug look.

She crouches lower and offers a foreleg. Her back is lined with spikes, but there's a spot between the wings that should fit someone. Trying not to think about how weird this is, I use her leg to boost myself up and climb into the space.

This was fine in theory, but I now realize there's no straps to hang on to like the grif squad has. Her head twists to look at me. I flip a thumbs-up even though I'm starting to feel vaguely nauseous.

I think Athina feels it because she climbs up the hill, pausing to kick the still burning spider corpse aside, and springs into a run. It's surprisingly smooth, like the lope of a horse I rode when I was sixteen. Then her wings spread and catch air.

My stomach still lurches as her talons leave the ground, but she doesn't gain too much altitude, staying a good hundred feet up and coasting.

Smart, since it'll keep us from being seen too easily across the Wastelands. Her wings barely make noise. I scan the ground, picking out some familiar landmarks. When I see the point, I tap her shoulder but she's already angling down, setting down just outside the ruins of a house that spreads over five hundred square feet.

I slide down and back away as Athina tucks her wings against her sides and shifts back. It's fast. Her neck pulls up and she sits back on hind limbs, then everything shrinks and tucks and she's standing there, human again, the last scales vanishing from her face. Armor and weapons still impeccably in place, though maybe a few strands escaped from her braid.

She rolls her neck side to side, eliciting a few pops.

And we're back to awkwardly staring at each other.

"How's it work?" I blurt. We should be sweeping the area, scouting, and setting up for the others to get there, but we're stuck in a moment together. I don't know how to break free, and I guess neither does she.

"We can shift as early as two years old." She tucks the strands behind her ear. "Though it takes years of practice to be able to do it so quick and to keep clothes and items with you." She's suddenly blushing, and I think I'm doing the same thing, like all it took was the mention of *clothes* to remind us that this bond is supposed to link us body and soul. Since I'm still playing extreme avoidance with surface level emotions, I'm definitely not ready for that.

"And the mindspeak thing?" For a second, I think my voice is going to squeak like an adolescent teen talking to a crush for the first time.

"We can do it as dragons with each other. And all of us can do it with our mate in either form."

That breaks the moment. "Fates, can you *never* use that word again?"

Maybe if you're from a shifter community that's a normal word, but I'm not and it's weird.

But she's laughing, a sort of unrestrained sound. I break into a full smile with the detached realization that it's been a long time since I've done it. A long time since I've felt in sync with someone in battle, though with her it's way more instinctual than with my old crew. I probably would have liked her without a heartbond, but this is making everything feel more tangled.

Scraping a hand over the back of my neck, I indicate the ruins. "Let's make a sweep before the others get here."

Athina nods. "They should be here soon. I'll take south."

I head north, hand on sword as I pick carefully through the half-formed rooms and rubble-coated floors, scoping out the terrain for about fifty feet outside the edges. All clear.

We meet up back in the middle of the ruins, back to sort of tiptoeing around each other. I'm not really sure how to ask if we're going back to how things were. Separate, talking only if necessary. Because things feel different, easier, between us, and a small part of me doesn't want to go back to how it was hours ago.

I can see the same thing in her face. It's winding around the heartbond that's trying to physically pull us toward each other. Instead, we take a step backwards with a bit of resignation.

Dejan was right. The amount of variables aligning to bring us together out here is staggering, but frankly, fate is an asshole and can go screw itself.

Fate took almost everything from me out here fourteen months ago, and is trying to hand me some sort of *firren* consolation prize with a heartbond I don't want.

The others arrive and find us sitting on opposite sides of the main room that's mostly sheltered on all four sides though open to the sky. Fallen stone lies in haphazard piles, and the eternal ashy dust coats everything.

"Cieran!" Remy strides over to me. I push to my feet and get slammed back a half step by him hugging me.

"You okay?" I ask once I extricate myself.

"Yeah. Hell, Sarge, you scared us." He smacks my shoulder.

Dejan stands back, arms crossed over the bow tucked to his chest. His chin tilts up, but the relief is there. Besim's hand clamps over my shoulder and he's looking me up and down. It's weird being surrounded by a crew again, and maybe I'll pretend like they know something about me.

"All good," I say. Though now that I've been sitting down for a few minutes and some of the alertness has left me, I'm starting to feel every bit of that tumble and encounter with the energy-draining crendrake. My right leg aches and it's spreading into the area of my prosthetic knee where residual nerves are spliced with mechanical parts. That's probably not great.

"How'd you get here so fast?" Besim asks. "Thought it was going to take you longer?"

I pause. There's no great way to say it without inviting some insinuations. So I just jerk a thumb at Athina where's she surrounded by her own crew.

Her eyes meet mine and I feel settled again.

The dragonwalkers come over. They're glad that I'm in one piece, and the guys thank Athina for coming after me. I pull back a little. They're making it sound like I'm actually part of Crew Six, like I'm not just here for the mission.

Her eyes flick my way again and I look away from it. Something like a question pulses through the bond. I shake my head and imagine shutting a door on it, closing her out—a technique for resisting mind probes I learned early on in Guard training. Looks like it'll be useful here, too.

I'm not doing this. Letting someone into my head, fight alongside me like we're part of a crew. Not out here.

No one seems to notice, except Athina, and she's got an evaluating look in her eyes that I avoid. Our crews start to settle, and I take a seat again. I'll set out my roll later. Right now, every muscle is throbbing and a sharper pain sticks through my right knee.

"Hey."

I look up to see Dejan standing there, weapons off and med kit in hand. I hadn't asked for help and he hadn't checked. But now he's here like he knows all my tells and is just going to fix me. Irritation simmers in my chest.

"I'm fine."

"Yeah?" He arches an eyebrow at my hand clenched around my right knee.

I look around, seeing the rest of the crew focused on me again. Remy crouches against the wall, hands loosely clasped together. Besim stands with arms crossed like he might sit on me so Dejan can check me out.

The thought sweeps in that my old crew would have done the same. I would have been in Besim's place, making Javi sit still long enough to let Masood patch him up.

"Don't think this is something you can fix, Dej." My fingers ease up around the metal knee. "You're not a warlock prosthetist."

"Yeah, I'm not an asshole."

"Hey." Remy flicks some harmless blue sparks of magic at Dejan.

The elf smirks. "Present company *in*cluded."

Remy rolls his eyes, but something really close to a laugh stirs my chest.

"Hey." Dejan's even tone brings a bit of calm. "A buddy of mine helps make these prosthetics, so I learned a lot about how they're made in case I needed to do something out in the field."

He still waits for me to make the first move. I'm usually not bothered by the prosthetic, but hesitation fills up my hands knowing that Athina is going to see. Half of me is wondering if it'll change the look in her eyes.

I undo the laces of my boot and slide it off. The pant leg is able to be tucked up over my knee where the dull metal meets with my skin. The burn scars there are turning the same shimmery white as the ones on my back and side. A good sign, if you want to believe the doctor.

Nerving myself up, I glance over at Athina. An impassive expression has settled over her features, and nothing bumps against the bond. She must have walled it off too. I focus on the leg instead. It's still sort of an eerie sight. Like the warlock prosthetists and the elven surgeons took my lower leg and cast it in something.

The ankle and knee joints extend and flex like my real leg, but I can't feel anything past some sensations in the knee. What was left of the nerves in my leg were spliced in with whatever is in the metal, plus some magical and medical jargon thrown in to make it work like a real leg.

So I can't feel anything Dejan does as he rests hands on the prosthetic. He says something and taps a finger against the side of my knee and again on the kneecap, and something clicks. With it, there's a *shift* in the knee and a surprised grunt escapes me. But it feels better immediately.

I flex my knee a few times. Everything seems to be in working order, so I replace the pant leg and boot. But Dejan is still there.

"Let me check everything else."

"I'm..."

"He took a tumble when that thing dropped him," Athina cuts in and I glare at her. She is unperturbed.

"Come on." Dejan waves his hand.

I yank at the straps of my vest, getting it off and trying not to show how it pulls at aching muscles. My sword belt and hooded jacket go next. The armored shirt I manage on my own, but Dejan's arched brow judges me plenty as a grimace contorts my face.

It's mostly just aches and bruises from the fall, from sleeping on the rocky ground, and fourteen months of days with muscles clenched unendingly.

Pale green magic covers his hand in a light sheen. He places fingers over my wrist pulse. Masood told me once that your circulatory system will rat you out, and most medics will go right to a pulse to find any hidden injuries. It takes a minute, then Dejan's hand moves from spot to spot, some of which I hadn't even clocked yet.

His healer's magic slips in and eases some of the pain and relaxes muscles all over. Until Besim speaks.

"Don't worry about watch, Cir. We'll take it."

I shake my head, muscles tensing back up. "I'm fine. I'll take mine. I know I'm not part of the crew but—"

"You are—"

"I'm not," I snap.

Dejan's face settles to expressionless. Remy leans forward from the wall and Besim's going to try again. Try to convince me that I'm part of them.

"I'm not part of Crew Six. My crew is dead. They're *dead*. And I'm…I can't do this anymore." Fourteen months press up and fight for release.

"I can't do the casseroles and the boxes of cookies and 'the kids are asking when Uncle Cir is coming over.'" I swallow hard and my eyes sting. "All their families get together once a month and they invite me every time, but I've stopped answering messages. I can't look them in the eye because I feel so *firren* guilty that I'm standing there and the others aren't."

They all look back at me with my cracking voice and shaking hands.

"And they'll want to ask me and I'm not going to give them some *bullshit* answer about how it was honorable or quick because it wasn't. It was bloody and messy and horrible. Javi burned, he *burned*. He took the brunt of the shot that got me. There was barely a body to bring back. Three spears through Masood before he finally went down. And Marcel…" I finally start to lose it. Tears streak down my face and I angrily swipe at them, but they're not stopping.

"I was conscious long enough to see what they did to him. Before I dragged myself over to the wild magic grenade and pulled the pin."

I'd tossed it just far enough to blow them sky-high and me in the other direction. When I came to again, I pulled myself over to Marcel's body. They said that's where the grif squad found me.

"And *firren* Andrej is still alive, so what the hell did they die for?" I practically scream the question, hands shaking.

"I don't even care about my damn leg. They just put a new one on, like I'm not missing three other pieces of me. Just like they think they can throw me into a new crew who can't find their own way out here."

Besim opens his mouth, but I jerk to my feet.

"Don't. Don't say the words. I don't want to hear it. I've heard them too many damn times *like I don't know they're gone*. Like I wasn't right there when they died. So just...don't."

I can barely look at them as I grab my jacket and sword. Stride out of the nearest exit. Trying to outpace the memories and the tears still running rampant.

10

ATHINA

"Damn." The elf tucks his med kit away. But Cieran's crew all just looks at each other. They don't seem mad at him, or upset. They just understand.

I slowly release the breath that had locked in my chest in the face of his rage and *loss*. I should have seen it before. It covered him plain as day.

My fleet all exchange the same knowing look.

"Will he be okay out there?" Iosef tilts his head where Cieran disappeared. He's left his armor behind.

Besim squares up his shoulders. "Yeah."

"Andrej did that to him?" I ask, anger starting to pool in my gut.

The dark-skinned human, Remy, nods. "Fourteen months ago. Cir's one of the best we have, and he's barely hanging on right now."

"Then why is he out here?" Dimos asks, with a bit of anger. We wouldn't even consider sending a mentally fragile dragonwalker out on a mission like this.

"He's got a photographic memory. Couple of missions out here, and he knows how to navigate around," Besim says. "And to be fair, we were only out here to see what dragonwalkers were doing out and about, not tracking resurrected personal demons."

There's nothing else to say. We divide up watches, no one mentioning that Cieran does not have a spot in the rotation. I walk out with Remy for the first watch. The pressure dip of a fire being lit in the shelter of the walls tugs at my senses. I check the gloomy sky falling ever darker, but there's no telltale flicker from the fire outside the walls. We split and find our preferred patrol pattern.

No sign of Cieran, and I hesitantly test the bond. It's like slamming my nose into a brick wall.

The hours pass quietly. There's no sound out to carry, no movement. I return through the small opening and nod the "all clear" to Takis, who takes my place. My inner heat didn't let the cold penetrate, but I go stand by the small fire anyway, taking a short sip of water from my canteen.

A jittering fills my muscles and I look up. Cieran is back. He's in the corner, bedroll set out, gear stacked more neatly, sword by his side. Even though he lies on his bedroll, face turned away from me, I can tell he's awake. Seconds later, he crosses arms tightly over his chest, and sets his jaw to stare intently at the night sky.

I'm about to go to my own bedroll when he moves again, trying to find a more comfortable resting place against his pack. I can feel the restlessness tugging at my muscles.

Frustrating bond.

Finally, Cieran turns over on his side, back to the low fire. I shake my head, casting some quick glances around. Everyone is asleep except him. I can't do anything to take the painful ache away, but maybe I can help him feel a little less alone.

I make my way over and settle down, my back to his back. He stiffens.

"Not a word," I warn.

A huff jolts through him. We lie in silence for long minutes. The jittering in my muscles from him begins to abate, my steadier heartbeat taking over.

He adjusts a little against my back. "I'm sorry." His murmur barely catches my ears.

"For what?" I reply in kind.

"For getting stuck with me. I'm kind of a mess right now. My entire life is a mess." His ribs expand with a sigh so lonely I almost reach back for his hand. But he probably still has them tucked over his chest. "And I come with about a metric ton of emotional baggage, so be even happier we're parting ways in a few days."

"I heard what you said. I'm sorry if we weren't meant to." I turn my head enough to catch a view of him from the corner of my eye.

"It's okay. Half the Wastelands probably heard."

My arms tuck across my chest and I readjust my head against his pack that makes a poor pillow. "If I lost my fleet, it would feel like my wings were cut off."

"Yeah." A sort of sob accompanies it. Ache and loss and weary heartbreak sweep across the bond. I squeeze my eyes shut against my own tears. "I think I'd rather have lost all my limbs than them."

Shadows skip and play across the stone floor, partners with the fire as it dips and leaps. "Do you want to talk about any of it?"

"No." He gives a choppy laugh. "I've got a significantly underpaid therapist back home for that." Cieran pauses for a moment. "But thanks."

I move enough to nudge my arm against his. "Sometimes it's easier to talk in a place other than a slightly uncomfortable couch while someone scribbles notes. The offer remains if you decide different in the future."

He gives something like a laugh. "You'd think they'd find something cushier."

"I've definitely complained once." I half-smile.

The silence falls between us again, but it's not a tense one. Perhaps it might stay that way after I ask the question pressing against my chest. I can't deny that something changed in the hours after I went after Cieran and then fighting together. And I'm not sure how I feel that it has changed.

"Are they why you don't want the bond?" I ask softly.

Some sound I can't interpret comes from him. "I've never been good at letting anyone close. Not for years."

I can feel it again. That deeper ache that underlies the bright pain still pulsing from his rage earlier. There's more than just losing his team. More loss that's *bone deep*.

"Why don't you?" he asks.

I wait, arms tightening over my stomach. I invited this conversation and it's one we should have but my reason seems...*small* next to his. Suddenly, I'm glad we're back-to-back and I can't see his face.

"It perhaps sounds stupid."

He scoffs tiredly, and an elbow nudges mine. "Anything other than extreme emotional avoidance is a better reason."

Now I fully smile. "I've battled up mountains and through storms to be here. My father is one of the most decorated soldiers we've ever had. Sometimes his name feels weighty. And I've done everything I can to stand on my own two feet. And this? This feels like..."

"Like someone is cutting the line? Trying to sweep everything out from under you?" he finishes wryly. I wonder if he can feel the emotion pulsing inside me. Or if this is what it feels like to him as well.

"Yes," I admit. "Like it might reduce me." This time my voice hushes. "Like I might have to reduce myself."

I have never looked for a mate before. It never interested me. All I wanted was to make it into the fleets. This is the place I feel belonging, where I feel strong, settled both in scale and skin. And I've long felt that I'd never find someone to stand equal to me. I have a good fleet, but there are some who don't like a woman in the fleets, threatening any prowess they think they have. No one's seemed to look and want the whole of me.

"That's bullshit," he says.

I turn to look at him, surprise filling me at his low words.

"You should never feel like that. No one should make you feel that."

The fire wavers in my sights. Maybe it makes it worse that Cieran is many things I'd want in a mate.

A "thank you" wars with a "would you make me feel that way?" in my mind. I say nothing instead, still battling through what I feel and what the heartbond is trying to make me feel.

From the beginning he's only ever looked at me like I belonged. Didn't question why I was with the fleet. No subtle, probing questions to check my ability. He just fell into step beside me.

But we don't want this. I don't want this.

"Go get some sleep. You don't have to stay over here," he says.

I try not to take his word or the abrupt subject change personally. Heartbonds and tangled emotions aside, I do know this for certain. "I'll leave if you want me to. I just didn't want you to feel so alone."

He curls a little tighter in on himself. The throat-stinging tightness comes back. "Thanks."

"Besides." I try to lighten my voice past it. "I don't think I'm going to be able to fall asleep until you do."

"You might be in for a long night. I don't really sleep anymore."

But he doesn't ask me to leave, and I don't move. I'm content to stay in silence, and it seems, so is he. Eventually, I realize his breath comes even and peaceful. I settle a little closer to him, and close my eyes, slipping off into sleep.

———

When I open my eyes again, the lighter grey of morning has replaced night. And I'm looking back at his crew where they sit around their small space. Dejan lifts an eyebrow, but they don't say anything.

Heat flashes across my cheeks. I'm not used to feeling a blush. Cieran still breathes evenly at my back. I carefully roll away and sit up.

Besim beckons and I join him, face still a little warm. I don't want to look and see what my fleet is doing or what *looks* they will be giving me. Takis will tease me relentlessly.

"He asleep?" the half-troll asks quietly.

I nod. I don't even need to look. There's a quiet through the bond.

"We're still planning on separating when this is over. It's not—"

But Besim cuts me off with a short wave. "No, we...we think it might be good for him to have you around."

It's not what I expected.

Besim offers a wry smile. "Cieran's tough. Life's decked him pretty hard a few times, and he always gets back up. But this last time...it sucker punched him on the way back up."

There's more to the story. More than losing a fleet. I dart a glance over at him, but he still sleeps tucked up on his side.

"It's his story to tell, but…" Besim shrugs. "Heartbonds are different. He might talk to you, might not, but just…" His hands lift again.

I think I'm understanding. "I'll be careful. I haven't known him long, but I respect him as a warrior. The mission won't be compromised, and I'll see what I can do to get him through this."

"Thanks." It's mirrored on the rest of the crew's faces. Remy flashes a small smile, and Dejan angles his chin up.

The warlock speaks up next. "We all knew him before. He's barely half-himself right now, but we hope he can get back there. If something works out after this, you've got yourself a good one."

The heat tinges my face again. I can see glimpses of Cieran, maybe the him from before. And I agree with Remy.

I excuse myself and head to my fleet. Dimos doesn't say anything. Iosef just gives a nod. After the cautions they gave when we learned of the bond, I was expecting something more from them. But we all know at some level what Cieran's going through.

He stirs slightly. I smile faintly as I feel the absence of the heavy fatigue that's been over him. For the first time, I wonder if a bond might not be so bad.

11

Cieran

A BREATH JOLTS THROUGH my chest. The others have been awake for awhile and I can't keep pretending that I'm asleep. At some point we'll need to get up and moving for the day. I lift my arm, still tucked across my chest, to check the time. Just before seven hundred hours.

My fingers rub grit from my eyes and I slowly sit up. The comforting warmth of Athina pressed up against my back vanished at some point. She'd been there most of the night when I'd woken up for brief moments before being pulled back to sleep.

A new smell sends my stomach clenching, announcing my hunger since I hadn't bothered to eat last night after breaking down. Low voices continue their conversations. I methodically straighten my hoodie and run a hand through my hair, putting off facing them all.

I risk a glance from the corner of my eye. The crew sits around a fire. Someone has actually cooked something and made coffee. The dragonwalkers are circled around another small fire with their own food. Athina is back there with them, but I don't look. The few words we'd exchanged last night felt loaded with something else.

Once I can no longer put it off, I push up to my feet, muscles still aching and a bit of a limp on my right side. There's a space for me at the fire, and I slowly ease down among the crew.

Remy wordlessly hands me a camp mug and the blessed smell of coffee rises from it. My hands slide around it, but I don't drink yet.

"Sorry about last night."

Dejan shrugs. "Sounded like you needed to get it off your chest."

Besim glares at him, but honestly the bluntness is refreshing. I'm tired of everyone, even them, treating me like I'm suddenly made of glass.

"Get some sleep last night?" the half-troll asks.

I nod. More than normal and I think it's because of Athina. The coffee is a little bitter as it goes down, but maybe that's just me. My stomach threatens to rumble. It looks like they pooled breakfast packs, and Remy cooked it up into something more palatable.

He grabs one of the thin plates and serves some up, handing it over to me. I offer a half-smile of thanks. They all keep eating and don't say much more, but it seems clearer among us. I'm first done though I was late to the meal. I haven't eaten this fast in awhile. Or slept so much.

I go back to nursing the coffee. It's been a few days since I've had any, though I didn't really miss ration pack coffee. Not exactly fine fae dining.

"Ready to get back out there?" Besim stirs a small pack of sugar into his coffee. The others sneak glances at me.

"Don't really have a choice, do I?" I offer wryly. "Andrej won't just lie down and die all by himself, will he?"

They laugh softly.

"Don't worry. I won't blow up at you all again." My hand scrapes through my hair.

"So what would you tell their families if they were standing here?" Besim asks after a moment of silence.

My fingers press against the tin cup. I know what he's doing, but it stabs at the raw wound. I knew Crew Eight in a way their families didn't. The way they knew me like my sister never would.

Dejan tosses some more sticks on the fire, and I watch the flames curl around them.

"Masood had to count his arrows three times before moving from a break or in the mornings." I trace the lip of the cup and swallow another sip, masking the burning in my throat with the liquid. "Javi was obsessed with frying everything." I force my stinging eyes up to look around. "Ever try a fried breakfast bar? It's disgusting."

Low chuckles answer. I duck my head to scrub a thumb under my right eye. "Marcel actually never went to the Alexandrian ruins." And never saw a sphinx like he loved to claim. Mostly because they're extinct.

Remy straightens in outrage. "Liar! I knew it!"

A broken laugh tumbles free along with another tear. I didn't know I had this many inside me.

"I was Javi's best man. Some cousin of his threw the bachelor party. We skipped out early and took pizza and beer up to the base's roof." And he'd cried thinking about spending the rest of his life with his soon to be wife. But she's still living along with their two kids, one of whom had a birthday party three days ago. Javi would be pissed I'd dropped the package and didn't stay. But he'd also understand.

"Remember when someone stole one of the CO's cigars from his office and he went on the warpath?"

Nods answer.

A small smile cracks my face. "That was Masood."

"No." Besim sits back.

"Yeah." I half-laugh. "We snuck into the office later that night, smoked it there, and left it on the desk."

"You had some balls to do that." Remy taps the side of his mug and new steam wicks from the coffee's surface.

"We shipped out early the next morning before he got in." We'd dared each other all the way up to his office.

"Remember that team-up down in the coastlands?" Dejan speaks up. "With dickhead Carl?"

Yeah, I remembered that run with Crew Eleven. No one really likes them.

But Dejan's grinning and it's a wild sight. "Dickhead got himself some nasty bites on the way into camp. Their medic wasn't around, so Masood offered." Dejan's practically cackling now. "He gave Carl a *firren* laxative."

I jolt forward, nearly spitting out the coffee. Dejan slaps me on the back as I manage to get it down between coughs.

"He got bit at least twice more on the ass before it wore off."

Remy is almost crying from laughing and Besim shakes his head in light disapproval. I swipe at my eyes again, but the tightness in my chest eases a little.

"Marcel could actually make some decent coffee with ration packs," Besim says.

"I personally think he always cheated and used magic." I take another drink.

The half-fae, half-human was our magic user, stronger than most warlocks thanks to his fae parentage. Masood, the elf with Arabian heritage, darker skin, and a dialect I had a harder time pinning down, was our archer and medic. Javi and I were the two humans, but he had some low-level magic, a wicked sense of humor, and was even quicker with his knives. Sometimes had a frightening cold streak that he never let show around his wife or kids, but that we'd sometimes beat out on the mats or sit in silence with a few beers on the tower roof.

"It's not cheating if you have it." Remy tips a drink of his coffee.

"Says the guy with magic," I point out.

Remy concedes with a tilt of his head. I finish off my coffee and rotate the cup in my hands.

"Thanks." I encompass them all with a look. They nod back. Remy extends a hand and I give him the cup, standing and making my way back to my pack. Pulling off the hooded jacket, I shiver a little in the constant chill of the Wastelands.

I get the armored shirt back on, then the jacket and vest. My hands hesitate, then I reach for a pocket on the front. I hadn't thought about it. This isn't the vest I'd been wearing on the last mission. It had been burned as unfiltered wild magic tore into me. But if I knew Emma Myerson, the quartermaster would have checked each pocket, salvaging what she could. She might have replaced some things in this new vest. I just haven't bothered to check.

The zipper creaks as it opens and I slide trembling fingers in, not sure what I want to find. The edge of a photo bends under the pressure. Two pictures come out, and my hands shake again as I look down at an image of me and my crew, armed up and ready to go, smiles on our faces.

I've got my arms crossed over my chest, thumb hooked around the knife hilt sheathed on the front of my vest, the ballcap Marcel charmed for me on backwards and sunglasses tucked in a strap. Javi's arm is around my neck, sunglasses on his head. Masood leans on his shoulder, beard neatly combed as always, and Marcel beside him, spear balanced over his shoulder.

My next breath comes shaky, but at least my eyes stay dry. Or they do until I flip to the second picture. Even though I know what I'll find, the sight of my sister grinning up at me still sucker punches my gut. It was from a get-together with the crew. I'm in a T-shirt and shorts, both legs whole. She's in a tank top and leaning into me, no medicine port under her right collarbone.

We'd just come back from a four-month mission. Masood and his family hosted us at their house and pool. I've got a beer in my hand and am flashing a peace sign with the other hand because Shay wouldn't appreciate the alternative. But we're both there and smiling and she's alive.

Besim's hand drops on my shoulder. He glances at the picture in my hand.

"All good?" he asks.

I lift the picture. "Yeah. Maybe."

His grip tightens, and he shakes me a little. I'm nodding and sniffing at the same time. I tuck them away and heave a breath.

One more swipe at my eyes, then I scoop up my sword from the ground and buckle it on. Besim still looks at me, but I offer a little smile. Like I said earlier, I've got no choice but to keep going. Andrej is still out there. Once my gear is in place, I look up to see the dragonwalkers up and ready. Dimos meets me halfway. He doesn't say anything but gives me a small incline of the head.

Our maps come out and we compare notes again.

"There's another small settlement about two miles away. They're usually okay for some questions as long as we don't pull a weapon. Maybe even hand over some coffee packs."

"Coffee?"

"Not a lot of supply trucks out here." I give a faint grin.

"Fair enough. Think they might know of him?"

I don't know if he's avoiding Andrej's name because of me, but I'm okay with it.

"Maybe. This settlement's been up and running for about ten years, so they've got a good bead on what happens out here. Others might come in to trade and have some sort of information. Good a place as any to try."

Dimos looks at the map again. "Then about ten more miles until his old camp?"

"Yeah." I don't have to double-check the distance because I know already. The location is burned into my brain. I flick the edge of the map, unsure how to broach this subject. "Athina said she's a scout."

Dimos confirms it with a glance at her. She's just watching with hands tucked around pack straps. Some of the dirt has been brushed from her black fatigues, and her breastplate and weapons are neatly in place. She must have redone her braid since the flyway strands from yesterday aren't visible.

"Remy and she can take point for now," I say.

Remy comes up to my side and the bond skips a few merry beats as Athina does the same. I show them where we're headed on the map and they head out, Remy prepping her on what they might find this far out.

I fold away the map. The rest of us do one more sweep around to make sure all traces are gone before we file out of the ruins and follow in the scouts' wake.

Remy reports in on comms, and Athina is probably sending updates via their mindspeak thing. I think once I accidentally get a flash of something from her. I flinch a little at the impression of landscape that doesn't quite jive with what's in front of me. Iosef glances at me, catching the movement, but doesn't say anything.

The heartbond's getting stronger.

Maybe it's our conversation last night or the hours of sleep, but I'm not rushing to block it out right now.

A few extra tendrils of smoke on the horizon announce the settlement. Remy gives the "all clear" and we stop to fish out a few caffeine packs. I wasn't kidding. The dragonwalkers contribute some.

"Okay, we good if I take point?" I ask.

Dimos gestures for me to continue, and I lead the way into the settlement.

12

ATHINA

The "settlement" is nothing more than a scrap heap. People like to laugh at the dragons of old for being hoarders, but this place is a melting pot for anything mechanical in the last two hundred years. Or maybe it's just whatever has been collected from the remains of the last war to tear across the land.

Houses or huts are pieces of metal stacked atop each other. Smoke wisps from chimneys, and there's faint movement. The stink of the Wastelands obscures some of my senses. I only get the stony scent of trolls and the more earthy scent of dwarves. I sneak in among the first circle of houses anyway, checking around corners. The inhabitants walk around, a few humans interspersed with them.

I send these images back to Dimos and I get the impression of him talking to Cieran. The heartbond feels stronger today, and I rub my chest above the breastbone. There's less exhaustion and heaviness lingering around him today.

The conversation and laughter around their fire this morning must have helped. Once we are back with them, he strides out confidently. Remy ghosts off again to keep scouting. I have not been given an assignment, so I follow with the others.

As he gets up to the settlement boundary, a troll barks out a rough challenge. Cieran's crew hangs back as he extends a hand. My fleet does the same. Cieran keeps going and I take a step forward, unease stirring in my gut.

He keeps his arms out by his sides, showing empty hands. The troll, however, has an axe, and seems ready to use it.

"Is this wise?" I mutter to his crewmate.

"Don't worry about him. Cieran doesn't need to pull a weapon half the time." The elf seems confident, and his thumbs are hooked around his vest straps. Neither of the others have put hands near weapons. I file this information about Cieran away. I can't help but ask and try so very hard to keep my voice neutral.

"Really?"

A faint quirk disturbs the elf's cheek. "I've seen him take down a troll hand-to-hand."

I study Cieran a little more—he's average height, broad shouldered, quick on his feet. And I've already seen how fast he is with the sword and shield. He and the troll are talking. It takes a moment before I track that they're actually speaking troll. And Cieran seems very comfortable with the language.

Iosef glances to Besim, and the hall-troll just chuckles. "I'm fourth-generation American. The language didn't get passed down somewhere in there, except for the more confrontational words."

"You actually know those?" Dejan arches a brow and Besim shoves his shoulder. The elf just chuckles.

Besim leans a little closer to me. "Cieran speaks three languages fluently, and can pick through another two."

What are they doing? These details don't seem directly pertinent to the situation.

Iosef turns his attention to us. "He seems to be a good navigator."

"One of the best." Besim nods sagely. "He once got his crew out of a maze over in Crete with only the sun and one look at a picture from above."

I frown. That doesn't sound true. Those mazes are rumored to be nearly impossible to escape.

"Okay, he says no one's come through, but they've been noticing some activity farther north in the last few weeks." Cieran returns to where we stand, lighter a few caffeine packs.

"What?" He draws back a little as my unwavering focus lands on him.

"Just telling her about Crete," Besim says, but his voice remains just as suspiciously even as when he'd been listing Cieran's accomplishments.

Cieran rolls his eyes and shifts between his feet. "Don't listen to them exaggerate things," he tells me.

Takis sidles closer and even Dimos raises a brow in interest.

He seems taken aback by the scrutiny. "Okay, what did they tell you?"

"Sun and one look at a picture," Iosef supplies.

He scratches the back of his neck and red flares across his cheeks. "I also had a compass, a piece of chalk, and some paper to make a map as we went. Common sense."

"What are we talking about?" Remy jogs up.

"Helping Athina keep her options open." Dejan smirks.

Heat sears across my face and my fleet chuckles.

Cieran looks just as embarrassed. "Okay, *shilsa*. You're taking point."

Elvish is clearly one of those languages with how comfortable he is cursing in it.

Dejan only raises hands and heads off in the direction Cieran points. We skirt the settlement and keep on north. Somehow, Cieran and I are walking near each other.

"You don't have to put up with their crap," he says.

I don't want to admit that it only makes me more interested in him. "You really speak three languages?"

He frowns. "What exactly were you all talking about?"

I lift my shoulder, and his lips purse slightly.

"Yes, I do."

And he doesn't like talking about himself, apparently. Something he'd shown from our previous conversations. I change the subject. "You seem better today."

He squints up at the sun, which if he wore his hat correctly, he wouldn't need to do. "Yeah. Doing okay, I think."

Hearing him talk and laugh once or twice reassured me this morning in a small way. "You seem a little better on your feet, too. Or foot." It slips out.

Cieran pauses a half-step, then looks at me. "Did you just make a prosthetic joke?"

But he doesn't seem mad. Instead, there's some lightness in the bond.

I shrug, hoping I'm reading him right. "Should I add blunt to my list of skills?"

A smile swerves across his face, driving away some of the tight lines around his eyes. "No. It's refreshing actually." He steadies the sword at his side before sneaking a glance at me. "Does it bother you?"

He seems nervous of the answer.

"Why would it bother me?" I return honestly. He was injured in duty and should not be ashamed of it.

Something else eases in him and Cieran inclines his head.

I continue. "I smelled something odd when we first met, so that explained it."

"Smelled? You know how *weird* that sounds, right?" But a grin lingers around his mouth.

"Humans." I shake my head. "So sensitive."

His chuckle brings one from me.

I have other things I want to ask, but I'm not sure how or where to start. And a little afraid to ruin the way it feels easy between us. So silence remains and we trudge on, exchanging a glance as the formation shifts and we alternate who takes lead.

I think I catch a bit of him through the mindspeak when Cieran disappears over a short ridge to scout ahead. It's a sick feeling, followed by a glimpse of more ruined spires, but no immediate feeling of danger. It tries to quell my dragonfire and leaves me feeling oddly cold.

Takis notices when I shrug my shoulders, tipping my head to try to relieve the sensation skittering down my spine. But I give a feeling of reassurance back to my fleet, and march on, finding a new uneasiness in the back of my mind until we make camp.

13

CIERAN

I LEAD THE WAY to another small hideout, tucked in more ruins. Ragged trees list between remnants of walls, and one larger trunk stands petrified in an old courtyard. The thing I hate about the Wastelands, among many, many things, is how you catch glimpses of the past civilizations that once existed out here. It makes you ready to see ghosts along with the moaning of the wind around corners and rattling through branches.

My teeth grind tighter. A colder wind is picking up and the clouds have thickened. Besim grimly predicts frost and possibly snow. At least this site has a roof.

Dimos sends a look to his crew and I again get the sensation of words or feelings just out of hearing. I shake my head, like that'll clear it. When I refocus, my crew is looking at me strange, and Iosef has a vaguely knowing look on his face.

Dimos turns to us and says, "It will be cold for you tonight?"

I nod. "Yeah, but we've got gear to make up for it. I'm assuming you won't be bothered too much?"

He inclines his head, hesitating a fraction more. "We have a higher internal temperature which we are willing to share."

"The hell does that mean?" Dejan's tone isn't argumentative, just puzzled.

Heat creeps up my neck and Athina steadfastly does *not* look at me.

"It means we sleep closer together."

Yeah, that's not helping things. A faint snicker comes from behind me but I don't turn to see if it's Remy or Dejan.

Dimos also ignores the reaction, and continues on like no one else is grinning. "We pair up. It will be easier to keep those on watch together."

This time I do look at Athina. We share a glance of agreement that we're not playing this game.

"Okay then." I nod.

Before I can get anything else out, trying to pair myself with literally anyone else, there's a sudden shuffle and my crew and the dragonwalkers stand alongside each other, leaving Athina and me as the odd ones out.

"Funny. Real mature, guys." I roll my eyes.

Athina growls something in the dragonwalker's language and her crew just shrugs, smirking away.

"What she said." I jerk a thumb at her, as she crosses her arms and glares at the forces combined against us.

"So do you want the first watch, or the last watch?" Dejan's question comes with a grin that has me shaking my head again, trying to smother an annoyed sort of smile. Even the thought that it's exactly what my old crew would have done doesn't smack me right in the heart. At least not like it might have yesterday.

Instead I just flip him off, and claim the middle watch. Athina doesn't argue, still glaring fire at her fleetmates. Dejan and Takis head out for the first watch while the rest of us settle in to making our surroundings a little more comfortable for the night.

We've got the bare semblance of a door, and three stone walls with the fourth looking more like a mound of dirt held together with some stones. Besim chisels out a deeper hollow in the ground and I make a short expedition out for some wood. There's plenty of fallen branches and some to scavenge from collapsed trunks that have not decayed at all in the last few hundred years.

My attention is drawn over the hills touched by the faintest light from the setting sun. Out there, scant miles away, is the place my world imploded. In less than twelve hours, I'm going back to confront the ghosts—the dead, and the ones who should have stayed dead.

A faint rustle behind me has me whirling with knife in hand, but it's just Athina, not even blinking at the blade.

"Sorry." I sheathe it.

She nods and sweeps up a stick. "Will this bother you?" There's some hesitation in her words. It takes a second to realize she's talking about the sleeping arrangements and not the mission.

"You just might not get much sleep," I say instead, half-afraid to turn the question back to her. I slept more last night than I have in a while, but I'm not about to think my sleep pattern is fixed after one night.

"Does anyone really sleep well on missions?" she asks.

A light huff breaks past my lips. I appreciate the words. Not much else passes between us as we gather some more twisted sticks and broken hunks of logs.

"Cieran."

I freeze at my name coming from her, and slowly turn. She adjusts arms around her load, head angled slightly. The dim light still lingering outlines her silhouette.

"Yeah?" My mouth is dry for some reason, heartbond thudding harder at what she might say.

She breaks her gaze, scuffing her boot against the ground before catching me in the coppery glint of her eyes. "Are you ready for tomorrow?"

Another chill attacks my body. As soon as we have a fire going and rations out, we'll talk about the next day. Even if I had a lifetime to prepare for it, I might not ever feel ready.

"I'll be fine."

"Cieran." She halts me again before I go three paces. "It's…"

This time I don't turn.

"You do not have to pretend to be okay."

A scoff builds in my chest and the wood rattles in my arms. "Maybe back home I don't. But out here, we all have to be on our game. You know that as well as I do. I'll make it work."

I stride back into the shelter, ignoring the looks Besim and Remy give. Iosef glances my way, then turns to Athina when she comes back in. I don't see her because I don't turn, but that stupid bond awareness heightens as soon as she's in the room.

The half-troll says nothing as I dump the load and retreat to the corner, pulling my pack with me and settling down with sword across my lap. That'll change once we have to pair up to sleep since the temperature is already dropping. Maybe I can convince Besim to switch partners with me, but he'd probably just ask some deep questions and leave me more antsy than I already am.

Everyone seems content to leave me alone. Either that or they don't want me to yell again and give away our position to whatever lovely and hellish creatures are in this part of the Wastelands.

I start polishing and checking weapon edges. Remy and Iosef collaborate together by the low fire, collecting ration packs from everyone and comparing with quick mutters. Before I dare look for Athina again, her boots stop in front of me.

My gaze slowly travels up her lithe figure, and settles on her face.

"May I sit with you?" she asks, voice low. She stands light on her feet, ready to stay or go, whichever I say. It brings back her words the night before. *I don't want you to feel so alone.* And Fates, I really don't want to be.

"Sure." I scoot slightly, though there's plenty of room. The small invitation makes her ease a little, and she settles in to clean her own weapons.

The heartbond seems smug, comfortably slowing in my chest. From the sideways glance she sends me, it's apparently doing the same thing to her. But I'm not about to ask what it feels like for her. It's been getting stronger with every second we've spent next to each other, but I'm not fighting it right now.

And *I'm not looking* as she takes off the breastplate and starts rubbing some tallow-like substance over it. But this time, I don't want to just sit in silence.

"Can I ask what that's made of, or is it a dragonwalker secret?"

"Oh, I will certainly have to kill you." A grin tilts as she hands the breastplate over. It's light, sturdy, with a little bit of give. "Our armor masters guard the secrets of making, so I have no idea what it's composed of."

"Shock absorption?"

"Direct hits can sting, but it absorbs almost everything. Watch." She picks up a knife and indicates I should hold out the breastplate. I do and she stabs down. The sheathed blade deflects off the surface, and it wasn't a love tap.

"That's pretty sweet." I turn it over again. No mark is visible.

"Does someone need to teach you two how to flirt?" Iosef looks up from the fire. Remy grins at whatever they are concocting.

Athina rolls her eyes and takes the breastplate back.

"Cieran never got out much except for missions, so he might be a little feral," Besim says. I pick up a small pebble and fling it at him through the low rumbles of laughter from the others. Besim catches it and tosses it aside with a smirk.

"May I see that?" She points to my wrist, also ignoring the teasing. I undo the shield band and pass it over. Her eyes narrow as she turns it over and over.

"Put it on, then tap the rounded part," I instruct.

She does and the shield whirls out. A pleased smile spreads over her face. She hefts it up and down, moving her arm different ways, the firelight dimly catching on the coated surface.

"I like this." She pushes the band, and the shield compresses. Open and shut again, and then she takes it off and hands it to me. "How does it work?"

I shrug, fastening it back around my wrist. "By pushing the button." Her lips flatten, and I can't help a small laugh. "I don't know. I avoid asking dwarves anything about their craft because you'll be there for a year, and they'll still be talking about tools."

She chuckles and pulls a small knife from her boot to start cleaning. We fall back to silence, at least until the murmurs from the others take over the space.

"So...never got out much?" There's a question in her voice and I shake my head a little.

"Did you want the full rundown of every date?"

Athina arches an eyebrow, but otherwise doesn't seem offended by my argumentative tone.

My shoulder lifts slightly in apology. "No. Between bouncing around foster homes as a teen, not interested. Then after I enlisted ten years ago, this became my life until…" My throat tightens again. Her arm presses against mine and I look up. "You?"

A faint smile and she shakes her head. "No, I never had much interest in anyone as a young girl, or once I enlisted, and they became surrogate protective older brothers." She narrows her eyes at her fleet. But lightness sparks in my chest and it's the same love I had for my team.

"Yeah, never stopped Javi from trying to set me up." It's out before I can stop it. Her head tilts again. Confusion reigns for a second at the unfamiliar name and she doesn't hide her look at the others. A pang laces my heart at the understanding that follows soon after.

"From your old fleet?" The question is so quiet, I strain to hear it. I nod. Then because a more muted version of last night's flashpoint emotion starts to push against my chest, fighting for a way out, I take the pictures from my vest pocket and hand them over.

My knees pull up, hands clenching as she stares at the picture of my old crew. Staring at *me*. The old me. The one who had gone for years without feeling empty inside, only to get pummeled back to the way I'd felt as a kid sitting in the caseworker's office, getting lectured about behavior in foster homes. Because someone had tried to fill the aching absence that my parents and brother had left behind, and I wasn't about to let them.

A bit of dirt is caught under her thumbnail where Athina holds the picture carefully. She slides it up to look at the second one. I force myself to look again at the smiling faces, at my sister.

There's an odd, almost possessive feeling in my chest. It takes a second to realize it's not exactly from me. Athina, looking at Shay.

"That's my sister," I say. "Shay."

The feeling passes and there's something like relief in its stead.

Then the small smile fades from her face and she looks at me. Directly at me. "What happened to her?"

I don't ask how she knew. Maybe she felt that gaping hole next to the one left by my crew. Just to the right of the ones I had mostly filled in years ago after losing family the first time. I guess I thought somehow, I'd be used to it by now.

But I'm answering, maybe needing to talk about Shay in a quiet way, unlike the words that had exploded from me last night.

"Cancer. They...uh...caught it too late." I sniff, rubbing at my stinging nose. Magic can't fix everything. And stage four cancer leaching into the bones is one of those things.

"Damn."

"Yeah."

"When?"

"Last week." My throat tightens again, that everlasting grief pressing up in my chest, fighting for a way out.

Athina rocks back, staring at me. "Why are you out here?"

A strangled laugh escapes. Maybe at the same question I want answered, maybe at the relief that someone else cares.

"They needed me out here for the mission." One leg slides out to stretch in front of me and my hands fall into my lap. "She's already gone and buried. I don't have anyone left back there, so what else am I going to do with my time?"

A sound catches in her throat, a mix between that terrifying growl and sorrow. I might have just been imagining that second one. Her hand falls on my arm. I want very much to lean into her, because it feels like the motion could keep the cracks at bay a little longer.

But we're parting ways after the mission is done, so no sense in getting used to the feeling. I don't move, but I don't pull away either.

"I'm truly sorry, Cieran." Brief pressure from her hold accompanies the earnest words.

"Yeah." I am too, but that didn't mean it helped. My shoulders curl in a little. I'm not sure if I'm trying to hold on to the feeling or protect against someone seeing the raw bits of me.

"I'd like to hear about her sometime...if you want to talk about her." The offer stays quiet but still drives the exhausting stinging to my eyes, congesting in my nose and throat. I'm one word away from breaking down. But I haven't lost it since the night she passed and I couldn't get off the kitchen floor, just absolutely pummeled there by the *loss*.

I nod, jaw clenching around the potential explosion of emotion. Shay'd seen me like this before and had just grabbed me in a hug, not judging at how messy I could get after trying to hold things in for a long time. It had taken over a year after we'd buried our family before I finally let it all out.

I don't want to beat that record.

"Do...do you have family?" I finally manage to ask, vision blurring for a precarious moment.

"It's just me and my parents." There's a slight rustle and then a picture appears in my sightline. I take it, still trying to get myself back on track.

It's Athina and her parents. They're standing on some black rocks, sea spray jetting up behind them and water of the deepest blue I've ever seen spreading out behind them. She's holding the camera, a little in front of them. All three are grinning. She's got the same slope to her nose as her mom, and her smile crooks at the corner like her dad. Sun-kissed skin and coppery tinted eyes and enough joy that my own faint smile creeps out.

I hand the photo back, this time daring to look at her. She smooths her dirty thumb over the picture with a fond expression before tucking it away in a thigh pocket.

The question slips out before I can stop it. "What would they think about you being bonded to a human?"

Athina regards me steadily. "I come from a long line of warriors. I think they would like you."

It makes me smile.

"What would Shay have thought?" Her words are quiet, and the question doesn't sting as much as it might have.

"Well." I clear my throat. "First, she'd laugh—hysterically—that I got a heartbond. Then she'd have you over for her apple-pecan pie and coffee and would really like you. Probably pull out her hoard of embarrassing stories about us growing up."

Athina smiles gently. "Tell me more about this pie."

I chuckle softly. "Add a little bourbon in there, and—" I click my tongue.

She closes her eyes, imagining it. "Sounds heavenly."

"You have a favorite?" I ask.

"Lemon." She rests her head back against the wall. "But it's even better fried with some ice cream melting over the top."

I shake my head. "How do you expect me to go eat whatever they're cooking over there when you keep talking like this?"

She laughs, and it lightens every corner of her angular face. The heart-bond grows warmer. At least it's stopped hopping around like a damn ninja if I look at her longer than two seconds.

On cue, Remy announces that food is ready. We pack away our kits and buckle weapons back on before heading over. He and Iosef look pleased at whatever they've put together—some combination of meat from the dragonwalker packs, rice from ours, and a better blend of seasoning than either had to start with. They start dishing up and I don't mind that Athina takes a seat next to me again.

Dimos steps to the opening and whistles low. Takis appears first, taking the plate he is handed and eating quickly in the opening before handing it back. Dejan is next, scarfing down the food and dumping the plate by the fire.

"Disgusting," he says.

Remy flips him off with a grin. The elf chuckles before heading back out to watch. The food is in the ballpark of good, but now I really want pie. I'm definitely not going to suggest that to the ration crew because I don't want to get some sort of rehydrated pie pack.

We clean up with compostable wipes and bury it all. The dragonwalkers have similar gear, though they just incinerate it all with a brief touch.

Another signal from Dimos, and Takis and Dejan come back to stand in the door, facing half-out. Dimos and I get out maps and tablets. I move closer to the captain and Athina settles her sword in her lap.

"We're about three miles out from Andrej's last camp," I start, my voice coming even, but my stomach is already compacting uncomfortably around dinner. "Last time there were some traps to look out for. We dismantled as we went, but I think I can get us back on that path."

Athina's eyes flit to me as I say this, and hers aren't the only ones. My crew and even the dragonwalkers look at me like I might have developed some new fragility with the words.

"If I lie down on the ground in a fetal position, walk around me and keep going."

There's some light chuckles at the poor joke.

"Be on the lookout for things as simple as tripwires. They also had plenty of magic traps out, so we're going to need the casters to stay sharp."

Iosef and Remy nod.

"What's your best guess at his numbers?" I ask Dimos.

The dragonwalker frowns. "We positively identified at least twelve, but intel suggests there's between three and four more in the gang."

"Roger that." I once knew every detail of Andrej's organization, and now I've got nothing. But power-hungry criminals don't change too much. "He used to keep higher level casters in his immediate circles."

Dimos confirms with a nod. "Seven of those twelve are at least level two."

Great. They'll be packing high-powered spells and innate magic. And Andrej didn't become a powerful sorcerer by sitting on his ass.

From there it's a standard plan. Advance scouts to see if they're even there, flank maneuver, then stealthily take out whoever we can on the way in. Find Andrej, subdue, clean up whatever else we can, and get out.

Nods come from all around. We splice together the crews' different styles to make it work. It sounds good on the surface, but we'll prep tonight and tomorrow for every little thing that could go wrong.

I share around the location of the hideout just in case, plus primary and secondary locations to fall back to if needed—coordinates I remember from last time I was out here. Besim preps messages to send back to headquarters for whatever the results are, and gets one ready to alert the grif squad if it all goes to hell. The dragonwalkers apparently do have some sort of long-range communication other than mindspeak—something more secure than a mind if a soldier gets captured. But it's tech based and still not working right out here.

From there it's turn in to get whatever sleep we can. For me this means sleeping for three hours and then hopefully not keeping Athina awake the rest of the night after we get back in from watch. She doesn't say anything as we settle down in bedrolls set close to each other. I roll on my side, back to her, a bit of warmth slowly creeping through the bedroll and my layers. Then a more real heat is up against my back. I don't move away, just taking a deeper breath for the first time all evening and shutting my eyes. I'll deal with the looks from the others in the morning. Right now, I feel almost comfortable.

14

CIERAN

I WAKE WITH FAMILIAR knots in my stomach. I'd fallen asleep after coming back in from watch. It probably had nothing to do with the living furnace at my back.

Breakfast is a protein bar since it's generally advised to have more than coffee before combat. The dragonwalkers offer to heat up some water for coffee, but I can't take them up on it since I can barely get food down. The others do, but I keep my hands busy at least with checking and re-checking equipment, until finally I just drop to a crouch, hands hooked in the vest collar, trying to regulate my breathing in the therapist-approved pattern. Because I'm about five seconds from a panic attack. My heart hammers, and I can't get a full breath over the dam that's appeared in my chest, blocking all but the upper part of my lungs.

I don't know if I can go back to where my crew died and face off with Andrej again.

A hand drops on my shoulder, and my eyes jerk open. Besim squats in front of me and doesn't relinquish his hold. Rustles mark the rest of the crew coming over. Remy mimics our position and Dejan stands nearby. They're all looking at me with understanding and no sympathy.

I wait for the tepid words of reassurance but they don't come. Instead it's just looks and nods. Wordless promises that they have my back and they know I've got theirs no matter what I feel at the moment.

It helps my ribs expand a little more with the next inhale. Besim's other fist taps me gently on the chest, right over the pocket with the picture of my old crew. I nod, acknowledging it.

We're all in for them. We'll make sure Crew Eight can finally rest easy. His hand extends. My palm collides with his and he helps pull me to my feet, waiting until I'm a little steadier. The others file by, fists tapping my shoulder and chest.

An extra pulse of my heart brings my attention to Athina. She dips her chin, the same promise in the action.

She deserves the *firren* world for not turning tail from me and my mess.

The dragonwalker fleet tap their chests. They've probably got their own memories they're fighting for, reasons to bring Andrej in. At least they're not voting to leave me behind.

I pull my cap on backwards, feeling a brief tinge of annoyed humor from Athina. A faint smile tugs my lips as I lead the way out.

Remy and Athina vanish ahead of us to start the scouting sweep. The rest of us trudge along the wider path that might have once been a paved road, ashy hills rolling away on either side, waiting for the signals through comms or mindlinks.

Fifty feet off the left side of the road, skeletal trees rise to the sky. The bleached white trunks are ramrod straight and withered branches wave in warning that whatever is inside the former forest is better left undisturbed.

Remy reports back first, one tap through the comms alerting us. I halt and send two taps back.

"I've got smoke." Remy's voice comes low through the earpiece.

"How far out are you?" I ask, trembling hand clenching around my broadsword.

"Half a mile. I haven't hit anything so far, but looks like I've found your last marker."

I swallow hard. The last marker we'd left before it all went to hell. A quick review through memories I hadn't really wanted to unearth, and then I speak again. "Okay, you should be coming up on a small rise."

Remy confirms.

"Get up there and see what you can find. We got a good read on the hideout from there."

A tap confirms again, then the comms fall silent. I pass it on to Dimos, and Takis's eyes close for a moment. I get a faint buzz in the back of my head as something answers. I try not to push back through the bond to Athina.

"She has seen two sentries so far and is clocking the same smoke now."

Besim shifts between his feet. Dejan cracks his neck and runs a thumb along his bowstring. I'm unconsciously sliding the knife on my vest in and out of the sheath. The dragonwalkers are doing the same small motions. Hands twitching, getting ready.

Another report comes through. "Counting at least eight. They're moving equipment out. Looks like there's not much left of any structure."

I suck in a breath, eyes squeezing shut before I open them back to the grey sky and the present. "Any...any sign of Andrej?"

But Dimos's savage voice interrupts. "'Thina's got him in her sights."

My heart smashes against my ribs, and Besim has to pass the intel on to Remy.

"Ready to get this *sunkata*?" Dejan asks.

I nod, jaw clenching and hand settling around my sword hilt. "Move out."

Every step forward is littered with memories. Besim's boots turn into Javi's even tread beside me. A faint rattle is Masood's arrows before he silences them. Marcel is somewhere ahead of us and not Remy. It's just me who's different this time. Almost like I can't remember how to get my limbs to move the right way: confident, unafraid as adrenaline ramps up, ready to be released in action.

A sensation comes through the bond. Satisfaction. I know one sentry is down to Athina's blade.

Two taps through the comm. Remy has taken care of another.

Crew and fleet nod to each other and we spread out as planned, coming at the camp from several different directions. Steadiness pulses through the bond, slowing my racing heart. I can't see Athina, but I'll take the reassurance she's sending. We get to the rise, and I brace myself to look over.

The Wastelands are even more ravaged in front of me—blackened stones and craters carved out. The smoke isn't from wild magic freshly detonated. It's from a stack of something burning in the corner of the remnant building. A battered transport is loaded with boxes, and several more men are coming out with more equipment.

Quiet lingers over the comms. As officer in charge of the mission, I have to give the go-ahead. I hesitate until the moment I see him. Wide shoulders, arrogant, wearing the same knee-length jacket over military-style pants and boots. Red hair, smug superiority, and magic that causes chaos.

"Move in."

Dimos passes the order to his fleet and we surge to action.

Dejan kneels on the rise and his bowstring sings. Two men fall before Andrej reacts. Fury twists his broad features, and he whirls to face us. He grabs a cord hanging from his neck and rips it off, shouting elvish words as he does. Sickly green magic coils, hammering into Remy's glimmering defensive shield. It gives us cover to get down the hill, weapons drawn, to slam into them.

Fire blasts on my left—the dragonwalkers wielding flames and swords.

The snap of magic flying back and forth fills my ears. It tries to send me reeling back into a different day of confusion and dirt and magic. But the very real human coming at me with sword raised is enough to keep me in the present.

I take the first strike on my shield to a dull clang, then it falls to hacking and dodging until the enemy finally goes down. Besim fights off two sword-wielders in tac vests and I race to help. We neutralize them in short order and turn to find a new threat.

A wordless bellow takes my attention. Andrej's arm is coated in Remy's crackling blue magic. He yanks against the pull, shouting another counter-spell, but our warlock's face is tensed and drawn under smeared blood. Besim and I step forward as one to go help, the sight of a brother in need overriding the reaction to seeing Andrej.

Two strides, and there's a punch to my gut for an entirely different reason. Athina is down.

A ground trap has her wrapped in scaled tentacles, more snaking out around her every time she manages to shake one loose. Something tightens within me. I need to help her.

"Bes! Split."

But he's already noticed I'm not beside him anymore.

"I got it!" He sprints to help Remy.

I bolt to Athina, sliding to my knees and striking down at the roiling mess with my sword. Her arms are pinned to her sides and scales streak her face, trying to shift to get out of it but not quite managing. Her eyes meet mine, flaming copper and furious that she's stuck.

"Use fire!" I yell, swinging again. Tentacles recoil, hissing as they start trying to snare me now.

"No good!" she returns, kicking at a larger one trying to wrap around her leg.

I swat one midair with my shield, trying to find the origin.

"Under me!" she says, answering the question I've barely thought.

The tentacles I've sliced through are growing back, and this time they have spikes. Profanity escapes as one gets past my guard and slams into my vest, not puncturing it, but knocking me back a little.

I ditch the sword, pulling my favorite knife instead. Athina starts trying to twist, giving me space to get underneath her. One more curse and I throw the shield up to protect us both while I get beside her and shove my arm underneath and start probing with the knife.

The trap starts squealing and smashing at any available limb or shield.

"Cieran!" Her sharp voice sends me twisting to see a troll looming over us, warclub raised. But we're both stuck. All I've got is the shield for as long as it lasts. The blow never comes as Takis jumps over us, taking on the club-wielder. Her relief burns as intensely as my own, and I turn back to my task.

There's not enough space. I jam my knife as well as I can, trying to find the trap center and kill it. Spikes deflect off the shield and slice across my shoulder. Athina growls, and warmth grows around us.

Tentacles tighten, then shiver, and pounding attacks resume. I'm close.

"Hang on!" I jolt the knife a little more to the left and it sinks into something soft. She's able to move, twisting away from me. I take the extra space and wrench the dagger.

One last shriek and the tentacles go limp. Athina pulls away, getting to her feet. I scramble back as flame builds around her palms and she incinerates the thing. I lower my shield after the initial blast. She's got sword in hand again. I sheathe the knife and scoop up my blade.

Takis is at our side again, saying something to Athina in their language. She nods and they face off with more opponents. I push to my feet, losing my balance as a rumble tears through the earth.

Pressure builds in my ears and *pops*. Remy and Besim fly through the air away from Andrej's outstretched hands. They hit the ground and don't move.

A sound rips from my chest and I charge Andrej, not really caring that he could hit me with the same thing, or worse. He thrusts out a hand. I twist away from the snarling green bolt.

His scowl fades as I get closer and recognition dawns. "You. Still alive."

I barely hear the words, blood roaring in my ears. I slam into him and we both go down. I roll to my feet first, setting my guard.

He's up and pulling a slender blade. Fury builds hotter as I recognize Javi's sword.

"You like it?" he taunts, swinging the blade back and forth.

My rage takes over and I attack. I block the first grey-tinted spell with my shield, its warding runes dissipating the magic around me. Time to see how good he is with a blade. Casting usually requires hands and if he's too busy using a sword, he has less magic to throw at me.

Andrej is not as elegant with the sword as Javi, his fighting and casting style closer to brute force, but he's still efficient. I twist around or shield block the spells he does manage. A few get through the wards and the shield heats dangerously. He's also clever, because he's leading me forward and I don't care until caution slams into me. The emotion has a crisp edge to it, shoved there by Athina.

My teeth grit, trying to shake off the feeling, fight back until it's just me and my rage and Andrej dying on my sword. I'm done with heartbonds, done with loss, done with the smug bastard in front of me.

An arrow zings by his head and he blasts off a magic bolt back, giving me an opening. He parries just as quick. His lips move and the earth shifts under me, sending me stumbling. Andrej slams his sword into my raised shield and I hit the ground.

A deep roar makes him pause, and I crane my head up. A black-scaled dragon faces off with a chimera the size of a draft horse. Backs arch and wings spread, heartbeats away from unleashing fire and poison all around.

A green-scaled dragon joins the standoff, tail lashing and decimating a stack of crates. The chimera backs away, lion claws digging into the ground. Andrej curses above me and I barely get my shield back up to block another blow.

My shield arm is pressed against my chest. Something tightens over me, pinning me to the ground as Andrej steps away. There's mass chaos in the wake of the dragons appearing and *I can't get up.*

Sudden light casts wiggling shadows, and another furious cry erupts from me. Silver magic swirls in a circle six feet in diameter. The magic sparks more colors, coalescing at the center before withdrawing to show a different part of the Wastelands on the other side.

Andrej is building a gate to get himself and as many men as can get through out of here, retreating somewhere we won't be able to find until it's too damn late to stop him again.

I try to get up, but I'm wrapped up tighter and tighter by his spell with each movement.

Footsteps and shouts surround me, and then Athina appears, knife stabbing down at the constrictor trap binding me.

"Stop him!" I yell, but she grimly keeps prying me free. "Athina!" I'm almost begging.

A snap and then I'm free. I wrench to my hands and knees as minions race through the portal. Andrej stands there, hand outstretched to keep it open, a smirk on his face as he protects himself from arrows pinging off an invisible shield.

I shove up to my feet. Then something tackles me from behind. Claws latch onto my vest as my knees buckle under the hit. Athina's surprised cry and shock pierces through the heartbond. The sudden impact stunned me enough that I can't fight back. I'm dragged forward, sliding through the opening and dumped on the other side.

15

ATHINA

A MUSTY-SCENTED WING CURLS around me, pushing me into Cieran. Bright light flashes in my periphery. Air pressure dips for one startling second before a punch flings me away from him. I slam face-first into the ground, something heavy on my back crushing me into the coarse earth and robbing me of breath. The smell of smoke, blood, and magic fills my nose. Weight lets up and I move. Shouting starts again, and hands grab at me.

I can't feel my fleetmates, but I can feel…

I move my head enough to see Cieran. He's on the ground, the chimera's front paws on his back, keeping him pinned. He struggles until its growl stills him.

"Hold her down!"

I'm swarmed by four men. Already on the ground, there's not much more to do than kick and punch in desperation. But there's too many to effectively fight back. Fear, barely quelled, rushes over me as my limbs are secured. A whisper of steel presses to my neck, further quieting the fight jerking through me. Andrej appears in my field of vision.

"If you try to shift, that knife is going right through you." His smugness is tempered by a shortness of breath, and he wrings out his hands from the magic he's done to create the portal. Black fades from his eyes from the stolen magic he's used, leaving them a lighter blue. It's the mark of a sorcerer who harvests magic from others and isn't afraid to dabble in darker things on a path to greater power.

"Got it." A man appears holding something, and Andrej smirks down at me.

"I've been trying to get a dragon shifter for awhile now. Thanks for obliging," he says.

Hands tighten as the man gingerly approaches. Too late, I understand what he has. A binding collar that will block my shifting power. Panic takes over. I can hear and feel Cieran trying to get to me, but I can't see him the way I'm restrained. The knife cuts into my skin. I prefer injury over what he has.

A silver collar clamps around my neck, sealed there by a magic charm. I'd happily beat the key out of anyone, but especially Andrej. Frustration leaks between clenched jaws. I refuse to let them see how the silver burns my skin, masking my shifting magic. It sends the dragon fire recoiling into the deepest parts of me, taking my connection to my fleet with it.

But the collar hasn't taken the heartbond. It's dampened only slightly. I still feel more than see Cieran's struggle as I am incapacitated. Some of the men swarm him, taking weapons. Then the chimera shifts back to a muscle-corded Graecian man with the nose to match. He hauls Cieran up like he weighs nothing.

Our eyes meet and my anger matches his. I'm similarly wrenched to my feet and our armor is stripped off and left in piles. They have to punch him a few times, beating him down to get his hoodie and armored shirt off.

"Leave their stuff," Andrej snaps at the man poking through Cieran's pile of weapons. "Any of it could have a tracker."

We're standing in empty Wastelands, no landmark around even if I could reach out through the mindspeak to my fleet.

"Radio ahead to Damien. Let him know we're coming in," Andrej orders.

An elf pulls a hand-held radio from the back of his belt. "What about his brother?"

Andrej sneers. "He fell behind."

He starts to open another gate with the same spinning silver magic as before, and my heart sinks. We're traveling again and now we really won't have an easy way for our fleets to find us. Gates leave little to no trace behind, no indication of the destination on the other side.

Is my fleet even on their feet? What of Cieran's crew?

The battle had not been going well before I got dragged through the portal by the chimera. My only consolation is that Andrej and his men are similarly beat. He's got six left out of the twelve who started the fight. It's clear he has some intention for me, but what is he intending for Cieran?

Cieran lunges at Andrej, and the shifter grabs him by the back of his shirt and throws him to the ground, stomping at him. Cieran evades, but gets hit full in the chest by a blast from Andrej. And I feel every bit of the strike.

He writhes, back arching, scream trying to escape. The magic fades and he's left curled on the ground. My teeth sink into my cheek, trying to keep his pain off my face. The visceral strength of pain is new.

The chimera hauls him back up, and practically tosses him through the new portal. I'm given the option of stepping through and I do, managing to move closer to where Cieran tries to get up on the other side. A hand clamps back on my shoulder, halting me. Anger throbs in my chest, but the warning prick of a knife against my low back cautions me against acting.

A few dilapidated structures list together and pits pockmark the landscape. Andrej steps through as the gate closes. We're now even farther from our fleets. Without mindspeak ability to call to them, I've never felt more alone.

"Now." Andrej approaches Cieran. "You're a thorn in my side I thought I'd crushed over a year ago."

He lifts a blade and the sight of the sword does something to Cieran. His rage shoots through me and reminds me. I'm not alone. It takes another man besides the chimera to hold him, twisting his arms behind him. Andrej smiles, enjoying Cieran's reaction.

"I will kill you," Cieran seethes.

"I admit, you came close with that grenade last time." Andrej sweeps the sword up and down, weaving a mesmerizing pattern. "But even dragonwalkers couldn't kill me. You're just a pathetic human with no magic, so what are you and your strategy and your three medals going to do in the end, Sergeant Cieran O'Donnell?"

He doesn't even flinch at the sound of his name and service record details.

"How'd you feel when you heard I was alive?" Andrej leans close again.

"Glad I could finish the job myself." Cieran stomps down onto the foot of the shifter behind him. The man snarls in surprise, loosening him just enough to lunge at Andrej. He almost gets there. I pull at my own captor to go help. But arms tighten around me, and he's hit with another blast of magic.

"Throw them in a pit. We'll have some fun later." Andrej sheathes the sword. We're both dragged to the edge of one of the holes, and shoved over the side.

I hit an incline, rolling and tumbling until I smash into the bottom, Cieran falling after me. Enough icy moisture has pooled to leave the ground murky and soaked, and just shy of muddy.

I land on my back, staring up at the grey sky, trying to shake dizziness and lurking nausea from the collar. A creaking sounds and I can only watch as a grate extends over the top of the pit. The holes are too small to fit through even if we could climb up to the top.

A groan pulls my focus to Cieran. He pushes to his hands and knees, then slowly sits, one arm pressed against his stomach. Mud streaks his face, mixed with splashes of blood. His trousers and lighter grey thermal are similarly stained with Wastelands filth, but at least there is no other obvious blood than his nose and mouth. The anger leaves him, and exhaustion takes its place.

"You okay?" he asks. I'm very far from okay, but given the circumstances, I can focus on the faint positives.

"I am in one piece," I reply. I hadn't taken any significant hits before getting caught.

He gives a humorless laugh, and drapes forearms over his drawn-up knees. "I'm sorry."

I lever myself up on an arm. "For what?"

Cieran stares across the pit. "I got stupid and landed us both here."

"Yes, I should have left you for dead," I try to joke but his hands clench.

"You should have left me and killed that *sunkata* before he got through the first portal."

Ire flares. "I won't apologize for getting a constrictor off you."

"You could have left it and then a lot of problems would have been solved," he snaps.

Problems. It would have killed him, torn him in half, in the seconds I could have taken to go after Andrej. I couldn't have abandoned Cieran much for the same reason he didn't leave me in the trap.

"Is that really how you feel?" I ask quietly, the heartbond that's only getting stronger helping me understand that it's only helpless anger and fear at being caught by his nightmare overwhelming him.

He slumps forward, digging a dirty hand through his hair. "It's just..."

I scoot closer, daring to lean my shoulder into his. We're facing opposite ways, arms touching, but Cieran doesn't pull away, not like he almost did last night.

"I know," comes my soft reply. Grief and anger can be scale-rending. I'm truly glad that we met, if only to show him for a short time that it doesn't have to be borne alone.

We sit for a moment. Suddenly, he sniffs and straightens, then his red-rimmed eyes focus on me. "Let me see."

He waits until I lift my chin in allowance before reaching forward. I hold still as he gently lifts the silver collar. Cieran winces with me as it snags on my skin, tearing at the tender burns. But its contact is broken for a blessed moment. He gently rotates it around, making sure not to let it touch my skin, but he doesn't find any break in it, no weakness to try to exploit.

"I think we might be able to get your shirt up underneath it." He glances up from the collar. This will be easier with his help. Cieran holds the silver and I tug at the cloth of my shirt, and together we try to maneuver some sort of protection between the silver and my skin.

We do a passable job, and scoot apart. But he rubs his neck in the same place my skin is burned.

"I think..." His eyes flit to me for a second, cautious of saying what seems impossible—*I can feel your pain.*

"I can too," I say wryly. My own limbs ache from more than just my tumble into the pit. But it would be unbelievably stupid to announce we had a heartbond to someone listening.

"Nice." He rocks back and studies our prison. "I'm assuming you can't reach your crew."

I shake my head. "And you don't have anything for yours."

An elvish curse is the elegant answer. But it encompasses well what we're both feeling. "Guess it's down to us then."

A bitter laugh escapes me. "I don't think I'll be much help." I flick at the collar, still stinging my finger with the action.

His direct and honest look has me oddly shy. "You don't need to shift or have fire to kick ass, you know that right?"

Cieran is right, though I still squirm a little. He's said it quietly, like that will bring more truth with it. But maybe he doesn't truly understand how I've always pushed and trained, trying to live up to my father's name among the dragonwalker fleets and carve my own place within them. Maybe he doesn't care about names, or proving anything.

Maybe he just sees me.

"And we'll get that collar off as soon as we can." He says it firmly. But we both know that's going to be impossible since we don't have the key, and I can't do anything without burning, and possibly killing, myself.

A clang draws our attention to a small iron door inset into the side of the pit. Andrej and three of his men stride out, coming straight for us.

16

ATHINA

Cieran goes rigid and I dare to press my hand over his in the moments before Andrej gets to us. Spears level at me, and the chimera shifter lunges at Cieran. He dodges, scrambling up to his feet.

I slowly move to my knees. A spear hovers in my face, just as sharp as the scowl from the man holding it. Anger churns in my gut, and I let it stay there. Some of it is even mine.

The air crackles and my attention whips to Andrej. The sorcerer's hands glow purple, warning in his face. Cieran is still tensed, ready to take on the shifter twice his size. His crew's words come back. *I've seen him take down a troll with his bare hands.*

But he's not going to do much against magic.

"Can't we be civilized here?" Andrej tuts.

A sound more feral than some I've heard from my people rips from Cieran.

"I've scried out your crews, but I need to know who else knows I'm out here." The magic crackles warningly.

Cieran does not seem in a hurry to answer. Neither am I.

"Well? Who's first?" Andrej lifts his hands, and the shifter sidles closer to Cieran.

The heartbond thuds resolutely, turning to something stronger, and it feels like a second heartbeat in my chest. It only strengthens when I look to Cieran.

I understand why we are bonded. There is a dragon deep inside him.

"Don't make me try to read your mind." Andrej shakes his head, but he leans forward, fingers twitching like he's eager to do it anyway.

The shifter barrels towards Cieran. He swivels on his feet, driving an elbow down into the man's back as he stumbles past. But it's enough to distract Cieran. Magic snares around his neck and chest, pinning him to the pit wall. Andrej advances, a hateful smirk in place as Cieran struggles, the magic winding tighter and tighter around him. I can feel the pressure in my own chest.

Andrej's lips move and a muted scream comes from Cieran. Something feral wakes inside me, dragonfire pushing back against the silver's repression. A rumble snares in my throat.

The sorcerer extends a hand toward Cieran's head, and I *will not let him* rip through Cieran's mind.

That's my mate.

Pain sears around my neck, digging through me, trying to choke me. I push against the threatening darkness, pulling on some strength I didn't know I had until claws burst from my fingertips.

My guards cry out in alarm, the spears wavering. Mistake. I bat one weapon aside, slipping past it before the man can react. My claws sink into his throat, and I rip toward the other guard. Grab the spear he tries to swing at me.

A roar comes from behind. I wrench around, coming face-to-face with the chimera's lion head.

Cieran is screaming now, struggling in my periphery, but it's a mixture of pain and fury. A flash of a spear-wielding human behind me flickers in my head. I lunge to the side, and the human and the chimera scramble to not impale each other.

I scoop up the fallen spear and charge Andrej. He's still trying to contain Cieran, whose desperate look falls on me. My arm slams to a halt mid-strike, and Andrej slowly turns.

Sweat beads his forehead as he keeps one hand toward me and another at Cieran, holding us both in a binding spell. My feet gain an inch before he shoves his palm outward, pushing me back. The spear is pulled from my hand, and arms wrap around me as Andrej releases.

The chimera slams Cieran against the wall, hand around his throat, pummeling his face and stomach with his free hand. Cieran tries to fight back, but he's off-balance, head spinning.

I try to shake my captor, but he's wiry and just as desperate to keep hold of me. The pain from the collar burrows through my neck, but I'm not about to let my claws go. The spear haft hits my stomach. I fold forward, my focus shaken enough to break the tenuous hold I have on my dragonfire. It flees from the silver and I collapse, writhing and screaming as fire burns me from the inside out.

Tears leak from my eyes, blurring the sky, the ground, retreating figures, as I try to get away from the engulfing pain. I'm grabbed, and my flailing limbs hit something sturdy. Cold presses to my face. A voice breaks through, and the agony reduces from wildfire to crackling to embers with alarming suddenness.

My vision clears to see Cieran hunched over me, face twisted in pain. It's his hand on my cheek, his other arm around me. Understanding flashes in, and I try to cut off the mental connection between us, thinking of a door sliding shut.

A *snap* ricochets through my head. He pitches forward, catching himself on the hand that rips from my face. His chest is inches from my face, heaving with ragged breaths. My fingers curl around his arm. I want to be mad at him, but only desperate gratitude runs through me.

"That was s-stupid."

He sinks back on his heels but doesn't let up his gentle hold around me. "I'm not apologizing."

I haven't let go of him either, needing his help to sit up. A ripple of heat follows in the wake of his knuckles brushing my cheek, pushing hair from my face. I chose him. Chose the bond with him in those frantic moments. The connection beats stronger in my chest, but this time I only feel settled. Perhaps I can blame the more emotional side fed by dragonfire, but I've only ever felt stronger next to him since the moment we first drew swords together.

Hazel eyes, lined with his own pain and exhaustion, fix on mine. "You okay?"

I nod. It takes an extra effort to unlatch my fingers from around his muscled arm. Carefully, I move away a little. I can feel that he hasn't chosen me, and I will still respect his desire to keep distance between us. He does the same, still wincing from foolishly helping me manage my pain.

Cieran leans against the rough-hewn wall, one arm pressing against his stomach. Blood covers his face and a new cut mars his left cheekbone.

"Are you all right?" I ask softly.

"I've definitely been better."

I scoot to sit next to him, a space between us that my mind approves, but the heartbond wants me to close. *I* want to close.

"You shouldn't have done that." My head shakes, but I'm not angry. My dragonfire is coiled back inside, but it feels even more restless, ready to burst out no matter the consequences to my body.

"You took a risk to try to shift with that on." His glance dips from my face down to the collar.

My fingers touch the edge of my shirt. It's long fallen out from under the collar. I do not want to know how bad the skin looks under the silver. I can feel it well enough. "Did he get anything?"

Cieran shakes his head. "We're trained to resist mind-probes. And you distracted him before he could try something else."

I drag a knee up, and tuck my arms across my stomach. An unfamiliar feeling prickles across my skin. I'm cold.

He notices and lifts an arm. "Come here."

I arch an eyebrow, and Cieran jerks his head in further invitation.

"Though if you tell anyone about this, I'll be forced to call you a liar."

A smile threatens at his light words, but I tuck in to him. The heartbond is smug, but that is not what worries me. He's freezing too. I can feel the shivers and see the way his hands curl to protect his fingertips.

"They'll be back," he says. "But I think it wiped Andrej out to try to hold us both like that."

I close my eyes, pressing closer. I shouldn't, but my body is desperate for warmth. Fatigue hits with a sudden vengeance. Trying to shift with a restriction collar on sapped my energy and the inherent magic that allows me to change form.

"Again with the aggressive cuddling?" But humor edges the words, humming in his chest. I tip my head up to halfheartedly scowl at him.

He adjusts and I'm face-first in his chest, my arms tucked against my stomach, his around me.

My eyes slide closed. I need to stay awake, help figure out a plan to escape, be ready for the next time Andrej and his men come through the door. But fatigue claims me.

17

Cieran

She's asleep. Pressed up against me, and my arms are acting of their own accord, holding her like I'm never going to let go.

Athina chose me. I felt it in those frantic moments pressed up against the wall while Andrej's magic tried to claw through my mind. And I feel it now. An extra pull toward the new steadiness and warmth that's her on the other end.

I'm not angry that she did. If the places had been reversed, I might have done the same. It's not just the bond trying to convince me to return the connection, to choose her, to reach for that solid warmth like I'm wracked by frostbite. Athina hasn't flinched once. Hasn't given bare reassurance or blanket platitudes about grief, or told me it will be okay someday.

She sat next to me and didn't say anything. Gave me something to lean on for a few seconds last night, and the nights before. She's honest, smart, capable, maybe a little reckless. Her smile and the way her eyes crinkle when she does is the best thing I've ever seen. Loves pie.

She's perfect.

But I still can't choose her because I got us both stuck here. What if I can't get myself out of the mental place I've been stuck in for fourteen months? I don't want to burden her with my broken self and watch her regret it.

Maybe when she wakes up, I'll figure out a way to say it.

Athina's body heat is enough to keep my teeth from chattering. The pit shields us from the worst of the winds cutting across the Wastelands, but the cold is everywhere.

The pain I took from her still lingers in my joints along with the aches from magic and fists that have slammed into me in the last hour. Most of the responsibility for being here lies on my shoulders. Solutions spin in my head only to be dismissed. We've got to get the collar off for anything to work.

And try to find a way back to our crews or get them over to us. We're gonna need backup.

Two hours creep by. They took my watch too, but I've gotten good at marking time without it. In that time, I get a glimmer of an idea. Remy is a good tracker, and can use that magic of his to assist for stunning accuracy. I have no idea if he has anything to help find us after being tossed through two portal gates. Those don't leave any magic residue and can be used to travel hundreds of miles.

That's assuming he's still standing after the fight. The visual of him getting hurled backward by a magic blast and not moving is still sharp in my memory. We can't bank on him to find us.

Athina stirs, pressing closer into my chest, a faint sound catching as she does. It's stirring me up inside, and I'm not sure how much longer I want to pretend that I don't want the bond.

She lifts her head, blinking slowly, a bit of confusion there. My heart stalls, hoping she won't freak out by having slept against me for so long. A sort of *mmph* comes from her.

"Sorry. I tried not to fall asleep." A yawn splits her face, and her forehead presses back to my chest before she starts to lift away.

I reluctantly release her and the perfect way she'd seemed to fit against me. We stay close to each other. For warmth.

"Doing better?" I ask.

Athina brings her knees up, tucking her arms between them and her stomach. She frees a hand to rub at her crusted eyes.

"As well as I can." She yawns again and it's weird seeing her with her guard down so much. Turning to something a little gentler, another facet of *her*. "You get any rest?"

A grin tugs my mouth. "No. Someone was snoring."

She pauses, then turns a pursed look at me that has me softly laughing. Athina smiles a split second later and her elbow nudges gently into my side. The smile fades to light concern. "You look worse."

"You really know how to compliment a guy." I don't really want her worrying about me.

She gives that same expression, her lips flat. I'm trying not to look directly at them. I cast a glance around the pit. We seem to be alone, and I haven't heard anything for the last two hours.

"I had an idea." I keep my voice low.

She doesn't noticeably move, but she is more alert.

"Before...I think I could catch a bit of your mindspeak when you were reporting to Dimos and the others. I don't know...you think you could reach them...through me?" As soon as it's out, it sounds unbelievably stupid and clearly grasping at straws.

But she isn't laughing. Instead, she regards me thoughtfully. "The silver is not affecting our connection. It is worth a try. It won't change much if it doesn't work, right?"

"Beacon of joy." I shake my head. But there's a slight lift to her mouth, a faint dimple appearing in her left cheek.

"How do we try this?" she asks.

I shrug. "You're the expert in mental communication."

She's just as wary of potential guards as she turns, unfolding a little to better face me. "I've never heard of anything like this before."

"Because it probably doesn't work?"

She shakes her head. "Beacon of joy."

I allow a faint laugh. Athina's fingers curl around mine, some warmth blossoming between our cold fingers.

"Cieran, I chose…" Her voice hushes. "I'm sorry, I—"

"I know," I reply softly. "But I can't. I just…" I don't want to break all over her too.

She squeezes my hand, no anger, only understanding in her eyes. The sight almost makes me take it all back. Instead I say, "We can talk about it later. Let's see if we can even get out of here first."

"All right."

A sensation pushes at my mind, fainter than when she mindspoke in dragon form, but I still recoil from it. Impressions prickle through, and the feeling of *her*, heightened after taking some of her emotions earlier and the ever-strengthening heartbond.

"Cieran?"

Despite myself, I jolt. "That's weird," I mutter.

Amusement hums back. *"You're supposed to be my—"*

"Don't say the M word," I grumble. A more audible sound of amusement comes.

"Think of my fleet," she whispers.

I don't dare look at her, to see what her face looks like with her words so concentrated. Instead I compile a mental picture of them from last night at the fire, and another faint laugh comes.

"That's how you see them?"

"That's what they look like," I protest. Then think of her in the grumpiest pose possible. I get a mental elbow along with a physical one, but there's amusement beside me and in the mental connection we've got going.

"You missed many details about them."

"Should I stare obsessively at them next time?" I ask and get another elbow to the ribs.

"Focus."

I return to the thought of her fleet. It feels like my mind is stretching uncomfortably. I wriggle against the sensation, and a muted *sorry* floats through.

She's searching. On impulse I start thinking about the miles of the Wastelands, trying to picture where we last saw them all. Her fleet. My—the crew.

And we run up against something. Athina inhales sharply.

"Thina?" A distinctly male voice floats through, followed by immediate suspicion and thoughts of vengeance and fire.

"Dimos," she whispers in awe.

"Holy shit," I reply.

She pushes a thought of her and me sitting side-by-side. Anger fades to surprise. I get a glimpse of our crews, all alive and bandaged up. Her relief churns alongside mine.

The impression of *where?* comes through. Her only thought is the pit and scant glimpses of the Wastelands, and she nudges me. I push through again, picturing everything I saw, memory still holding it in clear pictures—the landscape before the second portal here, the buildings, the layout, the pits, the grating covering us, the men Andrej still had.

Certainty rushes back and thoughts of airborne scouts.

A clang jolts my attention to the door. The chimera shifter stalks toward us. Athina lets go of me, but not before I blink away the double vision of the pit before me. The feeling of caution and *wait* is immediately cut off. I hope they aren't panicking wherever they are.

"What are you two doing?" the chimera growls.

I bite back a comment about his mom that definitely would've gotten me punched.

"What could we possibly be up to?" I say instead.

He scowls at me. "There's the taste of magic about."

I spread my hands. "I don't have any, and she's got a collar on."

A rumble builds in the chimera's chest and the acrid scent of poison fills the air. He doesn't believe me. Maybe he's smarter than he looks.

He lunges, and I let him haul me up by the front of my shirt. Lengthened incisors poke out from his upper lips. Ready to fully shift.

"I'll beat it out of you."

"Weird hobby."

His features bulge, the chimera pushing through. I'd rather not be face-first with him when he does shift. I jam my elbow down into the crook of his arm, breaking his hold. I kick his knee with my right leg, the prosthetic good for something as the extra weight of it connects with the shifter's joint.

The chimera staggers back.

"What is going on?" Andrej's voice cuts through, stilling the shifter's raised fist, but not disturbing my ready stance.

"They are planning something," the shifter growls. "I scented magic."

The sorcerer sighs mockingly. "He has none. And she is in a collar."

I arch an eyebrow, flicking a thumb at the chimera. "That's what I told him."

His rumbling growl hasn't abated. I'm not really a fan of the way Andrej still looks a little smug.

"I hadn't quite decided what to do with you yet. The dragonwalker will be useful. I'd been trying to learn more about their ways." Andrej gives an innocent smile. Athina stiffens beside me. The sound tremoring in her throat rivals the chimera's rumbling. "But Savvos is always restless. Maybe it'll be good for him to have something to keep his fighting skills sharp."

"Environmental enrichment." I nod. "Smart."

I'm really pissing the chimera off. Andrej smiles thinly. He looks tired, but he must have eaten a pound of chocolate and passed out for a few hours to still be this arrogant.

"Try not to get too messy," he instructs the shifter, then looks to me. "Maybe you can earn some food for the two of you."

Fareck.

Savvos remains in human form as he charges me. He's tall and his muscle outweighs me by at least fifty pounds. But he's pausing ever so slightly over the knee I kicked. I move back, dodging and blocking his punches. Then he pulls a knife.

I'm too close to the wall, so I pivot away from his lunge, coming around him. Another kick to his knee and it buckles, but he twists and swipes out with the knife. My dodge gives him time to lurch back to his feet and bull forward.

I catch his knife hand and pummel the blade away. Then get a knee to my stomach. Savvos tosses me a few feet, the landing compressing my aching ribs. My breath returns in frantic wheezes as he charges. I stay down, swiping out a leg when he's close. He hits his knees, and I lunge onto his back, trying to get an arm around his windpipe. An elbow crashes into my side and I almost lose my grip. He's trying to buck me off. I twist, straining to flip him over and get more leverage, but he's set and he's strong. A hand flies back, trying to claw my face.

Then he gets smart and shifts. I retreat, trying to get to the knife. I get a glimpse of Athina standing against the wall, Andrej with a hand leveled at her. Using magic to keep her from helping.

Shilsa.

A roar speeds my limbs. I throw myself forward, skidding on a knee as I scoop up the knife, and twist to face the fully shifted chimera.

I'm regretting the environmental enrichment joke, because I just became straight prey. He bounds toward me, lion paws and goat hooves tearing up dirt. He's fast, and I can't really get out of his line of sight no matter how much I try.

Swiping front paws and snapping lion jaws keep me dodging. At least he's slightly wary of the knife I have. He backs off after a strike comes dangerously close to his nose. My breath comes ragged as I wait in a crouch, knife ready. The shifter paces back and forth for a few moments before lowering on all fours, serpent tail lashing back and forth.

My mouth dries out, muscles tense as I wait. His pupils are dilated, taking in all the information he can. He springs. I charge, ducking under the outstretched paws, and stab.

A paw scrapes my shoulder, and a roar deafens me a split second before the tail smashes into my side with bone-trembling force. I fly across the pit, rolling until I'm face-first and gasping into the dirt.

Another bellow jerks my head up. The chimera has shifted back, tossing the knife away. Scarlet rushes down his arm. I can't even be triumphant because Savvos is coming at me again and I still don't have breath back.

I try to push up anyway, but a haze of silver flickers over my hands. Andrej snickers, holding me down long enough for his man to reach me.

The shifter's foot connects with my stomach, flinging me onto my back, and I get several punches to my face before I manage to block. Savvos hauls me up and slams me into the wall. A dim voice sounds and then I'm dropped, crumpling to the ground, taking another kick once I'm there.

Triumph bellows and I can barely lift my head to see the chimera, listed over with hand clamped to wounded arm.

"I smell it. He has a mate bond." His eyes narrow and he inhales deeply. "With her."

My heart falls.

Andrej smiles slowly. "Really?"

Something lances into my side, twisting and probing deeper and deeper toward my heart until I'm screaming. Another cry echoes along with mine.

The probe withdraws, and I'm left sobbing and spitting out a mix of blood and saliva. Athina is on her hands and knees, the same uneven breaths coming.

"They were trying to reach her people." Understanding dawns in Andrej's voice. "Start packing up. I can't risk them being successful."

"What about these two?" Savvos asks.

"She's still coming with us. So will he." Andrej narrows his eyes at me. "I want to kill him slowly for how much he set me back last time." The sorcerer sneers and backs away.

A clang announces we are alone. Reassurance bursts through me from Athina before smaller, gentler hands are on my shoulders. Helping me sit up, pressing against my face, tilting it up to look into hers. Concern shines in her dark eyes as she checks me over.

"I don't know if that was stupid or impressive." She gently turns my face. I'm sure I look as bad as I feel.

"Impressive, huh?" I try for a smile, quickly losing it as I move and the remnants of whatever magic Andrej hit us with zings around my ribs. "There weren't young dragonwalkers ready to throw themselves in a pit and fight chimeras to impress you back on the islands?"

She smiles a little. I'm getting used to the sight and about ready to keep making it appear for the rest of my life. "We have a sense of self-preservation."

"Yeah." I lean against the wall, my aching body curling in on itself. One of Athina's hands is around mine and I slide my fingers between hers. Our time is running out and before I lose the chance, I dare to ask. "Hey, when we get out of here, you want to go on a date?"

Athina's brow lifts. She seems a little taken aback. "Do you ask all the girls you get trapped in Wastelands pits with?"

"Only the cool ones."

Her grin spreads again. "Cool?" But she seems sort of delightedly pleased.

"Is 'cool' an insult to fire-breathing dragonwalkers?"

Shouts echo from somewhere—Andrej in full swing getting his men to load up whatever else they have stored in the tunnels.

Her hand tightens around mine. "Where are we going on this date?"

"Is that a yes?" A groan catches the end of the question as I try to move again.

"Depends on where we go."

I barely pause. It's probably the lamest place to take such an amazing woman, but it's the place I want to show her. A good start to setting my feet forward and acknowledging that I want someone to walk beside me.

"I know a great breakfast café. They have pie."

Athina's head tips toward mine. "I'm interested."

"I'll take it." I smile, and she's even closer. I swallow hard, taking in the sight of her. "Ready to get that collar off?"

Confusion chases the softness from her face. "How?"

Understanding shows just as fast in her copper-tinged eyes. I'm glad because I don't think I could have said it out loud. The idea has been there since the hours she slept against me, but facing off with it now has a lot of things tangling up inside me.

For this to work, I'd have to choose her. But I want to anyway. I've wanted to since she slept against me, since last night, since we fought back-to-back against those spiders.

So I do.

18

ATHINA

CIERAN CHOSE ME. THE knowledge hits with tear-inducing gladness, and my heartfire surges for the dully glowing embers that's his heart still lost in grief. He's the piece that's always been missing, the one I can be myself with.

He's loyal, fierce, intelligent, understands pie supremacy, holds so much joy that's been hidden away for too long. He makes me laugh and forget having to constantly prove myself. And is so, so reckless and foolish with what he's planning.

"Cieran, no." I shake my head.

"We can't wait for the others to get here. The only way we're getting out of this is if you can shift. So let me take it."

I refuse again. He only gives a sort of lopsided smile. "It'll be okay. Let me do it. I can't face leaving someone out here again. I can't."

That aching sadness emerges through his exhaustion for a second.

"What if it kills you?" Silver and shifters don't mix. Him taking the effects of it could stop his heart.

"Then don't let them collar you again." Grimness sharpens the lines around his eyes.

I cradle his swollen and bruising face, wishing there was another way. Knowing that I'm going to regret a lot of things if I don't kiss him at least once. So I do.

The heartbond leaps between us. His hand sweeps around the back of my head, holding me there for another kiss. Our foreheads press together when we finally stop.

"Okay." My voice shakes. Cieran nods. I clasp his hand and grab the collar with my free hand, wincing as the silver burns into my palm. His hand stays against the side of my face, thumb gently brushing the curve of my cheekbone. I close my eyes and call my fire, yanking it from its deep hiding place.

It roars up. So does the pain until it whisks away into his strangled cry. But I don't stop, heat building and building. We grip each other, gritted screams mingling. Brief hesitance fills me, vanishing with Cieran's refusal to break. Tears drip down my cheeks as I yank the fire higher. His strength is waning, and mine is about to fail when the collar snaps.

He slumps against me, head falling against my shoulder.

"Cir?" I toss the collar away, then try to keep him from crumpling all the way to the ground. My arms aren't quite working right. Pain ebbs and flows between us, and I pull in a shaky inhale.

"That sucked." He gives a sparse laugh. I cradle his face. Angry red burns circle his neck, matching the set I feel in my skin. The bleeding scrapes on his shoulder ooze a briny scent. Poison.

"Think I might sit this first part out." That faint smile quirks.

"You okay?"

He leans a little more into my hands. "Yeah. You're up, babe."

"*Babe*?" A laugh stumbles from me. "Anything but that."

His smile grows a little. "Hot stuff?"

A laugh escapes and I press my forehead to his. He's not doing well, and I can feel it. But I'm going to get us out. They hurt me. They hurt *him*, and my dragonfire is ready to destroy this entire place.

I kiss him again and he returns it with a bit of my own desperation. We pull apart breathlessly.

"Whatever happens, I am glad to have met you, Cieran O'Donnell."

A bit of red rings his eyes as his fingers brush my cheek. "You too, Athina Spera."

19

CIERAN

THE HEAT OF HER lips against mine hasn't faded. If I wasn't point-two-seconds away from keeling over into the mud, I'd be kissing her again.

I don't need a heartbond to be insanely head over heels for her. Athina's hands fall from my face and determination takes over. I want to help with this escape, but I'm not quite able to get my limbs to work just yet. Fire still scorches through me, and every breath scrapes raw.

Athina pushes to her feet, a bit of wildness taking over her posture as she tips her head side to side, taking in the pit and the grating above. Then she tilts a glance at me like she can hear my admiring thought, a faint smile in place that makes me think she actually did get a glimpse of it, but I don't even care.

One deep breath and she shifts. Red scales ripple over her skin, muscles bulge, wings burst, head shakes on long neck. Spikes appear and her tail lashes before it curls protectively in front of me. Her dragon form takes up most of the pit. Then she stands on hind legs, her claws setting in the grating at the top and pushes, wrenches, until it reverses on its track with groans and squeals.

A grumble builds in her chest, tremoring through the ground. Her presence in my mind seems larger and sharper. Shouts start up from somewhere. Her growl intensifies.

"Get on."

Her tail sweeps closer, pushing up under my arm. Helping me to my feet and to her side where she crouches to let me slowly work my way up onto her back. One copper eye regards me where I hang on grimly. I don't have the energy for any reassurance that I don't feel as bad as I do.

But she doesn't look for any. Instead rearing up and setting her claws on the edge of the pit. I curse and lurch forward to grab on to her neck spikes as she scrambles up.

We clear the pit. Athina immediately swipes at a man lunging with a steel spear. It's clear he wasn't expecting a whole dragon to emerge over the side, and I'm almost sorry for him before he gets batted away. Silver magic flares, snaring around her left foreleg and she whips around, teeth bared.

Andrej's feet brace wide in the muddy ground, hands outstretched, barely controlling the rope of magic as Athina pulls and snaps at him. More men run toward us, fear tinging their shouts. I'm beyond useless on her back, but that spear is just lying there.

"Don't even think about it." Her voice rebounds into my head.

"You want help or not?" I shoot back.

"Our fleets are on the way." I get a picture of airborne dragons, but I have no idea where they are. "On the way" could just as easily mean "too late."

Andrej and Athina are still locked in a tug-of-war. Men stalk forward, weapons lowered cautiously.

Screw it.

I slide off, keeping her between me and Andrej. My boots hit the ground, the impact making my knees buckle. Athina's frustration hits me like a punch. I send back an image of me flipping her off. She doesn't appreciate it, but I'm already staggering to the spear, scooping it up, and trying to maintain my footing.

One of Andrej's minions charges. The spear was always Marcel's thing, but he'd never stopped trying to get me to be a little more elegant with it. I can hear his voice in my head as I block a sword strike with the shaft, kick at the man's knee. As he stumbles, I change grips and stab.

Almost looked like you know what you're doing. Marcel's usual way of complimenting.

I consider exchanging spear for the enemy's sword, but I'm barely keeping the spear up in guard position. I pivot toward Athina. Another man is about to stab at her unprotected shoulder. He barely sees me coming around her leg.

She and Andrej still duke it out. She's free of the silver rope, and snaps at him. He dodges and sends bursts of magic that sizzle and flicker over her scales, some biting deeper to grunts of pain I can feel.

Warning flickers down my back. I whirl, barely battering away a sword strike with the spear haft. This dark-haired elf seems more grimly determined and slightly better trained. He's driving me away from Athina, but putting his back to her in the process. I don't want to distract her from her battle, but I send a brief picture to her when the elf is just in position.

She doesn't turn, just swipes out with her tail. He's flung twenty feet away.

A rattle draws my attention back to the buildings. A truck filled with six more men skids to a halt. They pile out, pulling weapons. At least two conjure up purple-tinted fae magic, and another spins brighter red warlock fire magic.

We need to get in the air, but there's no way we'll make it out with this many magic users. Dull acceptance starts to wash over me, unchanged by the fight still filling Athina. I limp toward the new threats. If I'm going to die in these stupid Wastelands, I'm doing it fighting, not helplessly blown halfway to hell.

Most of the enemy turn my way, but magic users are distracted by Athina's dragon form. Sudden fire drops onto the truck, searing heat blasting out and sending us all recoiling. A roar draws my attention up where three dragons pull out of their dive, my crew on their backs.

Relief overwhelms me so fast that I miss the chimera shifter. I'm thrown to the ground by his fury. Half-stunned, I'm barely able to struggle as Savvos hauls me up by the throat and shoves me to the ground again. His eyes are filled with poison and features are bulging, ready to shift.

I get halfway up on an elbow, boots scraping the ground, faintly conscious of the shouts and panic as our reinforcements enter the fight. The chimera's steel-toe boot comes dangerously close to my chest, air from its passing shivering through my shirt as I evade.

Rolling, I push up to my feet. We're close to the pit now, and I've lost the spear. Savvos has knives pulled and I'm searching for a weapon. He charges, and I abandon my quest in order to fend him off.

I really hate unbalanced hand-to-hand combat. Thankfully he's not great at it, probably more used to just overwhelming with brute strength. But unfortunately, he's really strong.

I dodge a swipe, but stumble on the uneven terrain. A kick has me falling to the ground. I grab a handful of dirt. Savvos bellows as it hits him square in the face. He reels back to scrub at his eyes. I push halfway to my feet again, freezing in place at the sight in front of me.

Andrej has Athina in a chokehold of black-laced magic. Her wings beat as one foreleg tries to claw at it. I feel each of her panicked gasps in my throat.

A black-scaled dragon swoops, and Dejan shoots two arrows from its back. The first hits Andrej in the back of the shoulder and the black-laced magic flickers. Dejan pivots on the dragon's back and fires again as they pass over. This one sears through the magic hold, sending some sort of green flicker racing toward Andrej. It hits him in the fingers, sending him staggering back with a curse.

He's off-balance from the arrow and whatever spell the second arrow was laced with. Athina's legs hit the ground. Andrej pulls back a hand, ready to unleash magic again. She lunges and her jaws close around him.

Bone-crushing relief crashes over me at the gruesome sight of Andrej dying by dragon bite. He's not getting back up this time.

The chimera tackles me to the ground. I twist under him, getting hands up to stop the downwards thrust of his knife.

His eyes are red from the dirt, and he's still blinking furiously to clear his vision. But he doesn't really need to see to squash and stab me.

My arms shake. The knife inches closer to my chest. The chimera frees a hand and I'm helpless as he smirks, pushing down against the knife, while his free hand shifts into a lion paw.

I try to shove the knife off its course for my heart, but claws score my ribs and a cry escapes. My strength falters. The knife hits my chest.

20

ATHINA

SORCERERS TASTE *FOUL*. I release Andrej's corpse, satisfied that he's dead. Dead and no longer able to haunt Cieran or my people.

A phantom knife stabs into my shoulder. Agony plunges into my heart along with it. I whip around, finding the chimera shifter atop Cieran whose scream *shreds* me.

One leap forward, and my jaws clamp around the shifter. One shake and satisfying snap of neck breaking later, I toss him into the pit. Cieran's weakness rushes over me before he shuts it away.

I shift back to human form, crashing to my knees beside Cieran. A knife is buried in his left shoulder. His back arches and there's so much blood. I reach for the knife but a sharp "Don't touch it!" stays my hand in time.

Dejan crashes down beside us. "Hang tight, Cir."

His hand presses to Cieran's chest and he grabs his medic bag with the other. Another strangled cry comes from Cieran as his limbs jerk.

"Shit. Don't move, Cir."

A muffled curse is his answer.

Dejan's hands spread over Cieran, light silver-green shimmering in the air and stilling him. "Rem, I need you!"

I finally look around. There are bodies everywhere. Takis remains in dragon form, but the others have shifted back. Dimos stalks about, weapon out and making sure everything is clear. But not even the sight of my fleet can make this moment bearable.

"Can't!" Remy's shout draws me to where he kneels by a writhing figure. "Bes got hit with wild magic."

"*Shit.*" Dejan whips back around. Cieran's face has lost all color, and his eyelids are fluttering. My hand sinks into his unruly brown hair, the other on his arm. Anger fills me. I'm helpless here, and I hate it.

Iosef joins us in a breathless burst. "What do you need?"

Hope springs faintly in my chest. He has some extra magic capability from a warlock ancestor. He can help. He *must* be able to help.

"He got stabbed with a hex blade," Dejan says. "That thing will work its way to his heart each time he moves. Can you do a holding spell on him?"

Iosef nods. His hands form a pattern before a brighter gold filled with sparks of copper spreads over Cieran. Dejan lets go of his spell and turns to the knife.

"What can I do?" My voice comes hoarse.

Dejan doesn't even spare me a glance. "Keep him with us."

My fingers comb through Cieran's hair, desperate to reach for his hand. Not daring for fear it might make something worse. My mate's tremors are locked in place by Iosef's spell, but I can still feel every one of them jittering through my limbs.

Dejan's hands close around the knife, flickers of green bumping against Iosef's magic. A faint burst of freshness accompanies it and just breathing in the scent has some of the tightness in my muscles easing.

I reach out through the mindspeak, but it's like running into a wall. Sweat trickles down Cieran's face and moisture escapes from the corner of his eye. I press in mentally and the wall gives a little.

I lean close to him. "Let me take some of it."

His refusal is bitter in my head.

"Cieran," I say softly. "Let me carry some for you."

A pause. Then a feeling a little like a door creaking open, and I get stabbed in the shoulder by a phantom knife. Something rakes over my ribs. I blink rapidly, willing strength to overpower it and send some to Cieran.

"Almost got it," Dejan says. A sheen of sweat covers his forehead. His fingers curl around the knife. "I'm going to pull this. Don't let him go."

Iosef murmurs affirmative and I brace myself. Dejan yanks and a scream still fights its way from Cieran's immobile body. The elf tosses the knife into the pit and grabs a bandage roll from his pack, ripping it open with his teeth.

"Dej, I'm gonna need you!" Remy shouts.

The elf pushes his hand, coated in green healing magic, against the wound for long seconds. He speaks some words in elvish with a Slavic cadence, then he wraps bandages over Cieran's shoulder. "Almost done!"

Relief trickles through the bond and the pain I'm carrying slackens.

"Okay, let him go," Dejan instructs. Iosef's magic fades and Cieran bucks against the ground, his cries now free to escape. The elf tosses some more packs to Iosef. "Get those on his other injuries." He scoops up his pack and hustles over to his other fleetmate.

Iosef and I lift a faintly struggling Cieran into my arms. I keep him as still as I can while Iosef applies gauze and bandages to his ribs and the still-bleeding scrapes.

My arms cradle Cieran, his head partially turned to me where it rests against my shoulder. His breath bursts hot and ragged. Every few seconds, tremors run through him. The door to his pain is sneaking shut. I gently stick a mental foot in it, keeping it open and letting me still help him bear the hurt.

Iosef grabs the heartbond dampener around his wrist, about to offer it to me. Wanting me to protect myself. I shake my head. I'm not letting Cieran suffer alone again.

"We'll get you home. Hang on, Cir," I repeat over and over, my voice gently murmuring in his ear, against his hair when my lips sneak close enough to press a faint kiss there.

Clammy fingers settle over my wrist. I feel him trying—trying to hang on. Iosef presses a hand to my shoulder. He knows I'm shouldering some of Cieran's burden and understands. He and his wife would do the same thing for each other. I nod reassurance I don't quite feel. Cieran is so close to slipping away, but I can't lose him now. I won't.

Dejan returns in a spray of dirt. His face is paler than it was, his pupils dilated. He is dangerously close to using too much magic to save his fleetmates. Dimos hastens over to join us. Blood spatters his armor and fatigues, and a few silver scales still mark his face and hands where he must have been hit.

"We need to get him and Bes back. They both need surgeons, and it's gonna take too long to get the grif squad out here." Dejan looks to Dimos. We all know what he's asking, and he doesn't seem to care that he's breaking propriety by asking us to bear loads. Even if they reached some past agreement to get here in time. But I'm ready to scoop Cieran up and fly him wherever there's the best chance of him surviving.

Dimos nods. "Send word ahead to your people to let them know dragons will be coming in."

Dejan's shoulders buckle in relief. Remy gets to work on one of the magic messenger tubes Besim had prepped last night. Dejan grabs a folded rectangle from his pack, sets it on the ground, and stands back with a sharp word. It snaps out into a stretcher with straps.

I don't want to give Cieran up. It takes a moment before I can release my hold on him enough for Dejan and Iosef to step in and lift him onto the stretcher.

"I'll carry him," I say before Dimos can ask. My fleet tries to protest. My body aches, but I'm not letting anyone else touch him right now.

Standing back, I shift, then stand protectively by the stretcher. Dejan doesn't argue, just beckons me over. I figure out what he needs when he starts undoing longer straps coiled on the sides. Remy cinches the shorter cords over Cieran to keep him in place. When he's done, I stand over the stretcher, lowering into a crouch.

Straps are tossed over my back, around my spread wings, and tightened. Cieran still breathes, and his heartbeat echoes alongside mine.

Takis offers to take Besim. The same process is repeated with another stretcher Dejan pulls out, with the half-troll secured to my fleetmate's black-scaled form. Dimos and Iosef shift, and the human and elf scramble up onto their backs.

We launch into the air, wings pounding the air as we gain altitude. Dimos and Iosef spread to protectively flank Takis and me. Dimos sends us course corrections as he gets them from the Drax soldiers. I follow the others, thinking of nothing but Cieran and the way his heart keeps fighting beat after beat.

Hours and hours are reduced to each beat of my wings, each echo of Cieran's heart alongside mine. Ruins, flattened ground, shattered mountains pass beneath. Finally a city comes into view. Three griffins come to circle around us, archers on their backs. I bare my teeth and start to angle toward the threat. Only Dimos's sharp flick of his tail pushes me back into position.

Remy sends a few hand signals. The archers acknowledge, but the griffins don't let up their sweeping patrol.

They accompany us to a tall building with a large red cross painted on a rooftop landing pad. Now that our destination is in sight, my wings scream in fatigued protest, wobbling the last few beats. We land. Seconds later a few more soldiers hurry from a stairwell inset into the roof. Takis's neck arches against the threat. Dimos's growl barely stills me from doing the same. Dejan and Remy jump down, reassuring in quick words until weapons are put away. The elf and warlock turn to us and start undoing the straps around Takis and me as nurses in blue scrubs rush out.

Once the straps are free of my wings, I shift, nearly falling atop Cieran. His eyes flutter open for a second, something impossibly like a smile twitching before they slide shut again. My hand finds his face, trying to bring him back, but exhaustion punches me from every side. Hands gently push me away and nurses swarm in.

"Who's got the heartbond?" one asks.

Someone answers. I can't lift my gaze from Cieran. A nurse slides a copper-inlaid bracelet onto his wrist, and another is shoved onto mine before I quite register what's happening. The heartbond fades in a rush, and alarm at the sudden absence of Cieran surges in its place. I snarl, lunging at the fool who dared use bonds on us again.

"'Thina!" Iosef's arm circles me, pulling me against him, reassurance trying to push in through the mindspeak. "He's got to go to surgery."

The wide-eyed nurse backs away. I can't quite find apology as Iosef's words finally sink in. We have to be blocked from feeling each other while he is treated so that I do not take any accidental injury. I slump to the ground, watching numbly as they carry my mate away. Another troop of elf and human nurses take Besim's stretcher after them.

"He'll be all right." Iosef's words fall flat. Pressure builds in my throat, trying to squeak out. I clear my throat.

"I know. We just..." I scrub a dirty hand over my face. "We had a date."

21

ATHINA

IOSEF PULLS ME GENTLY to my feet. I sag against him. My fleet is around me in a moment, hands against my shoulders and reassurance pushing in. I leave Iosef's support and turn to Dimos. Our captain is not one for hugs, but he enfolds me, hand pressing against my aching shoulders.

"Well done," he murmurs. He lets me feel the fear that he might have lost a soldier before shuttering it away. My bright relief that they are also alive and safe reaches toward him and the others. He taps my shoulder, and I tighten my hold until a slight squirm rocks him.

I pull back with a faint smile and he narrows his eyes. My knees wobble and Takis places his hand under my elbow.

"Your hair is a mess," he says.

I don't want to know how bad it is. But we both share some of the same vanity.

"So is yours." Muck plasters the side of his face and neck, flattening his curly hair along with it.

He chuckles and pulls me into a quick embrace, tapping his forehead against mine. "I also see I can congratulate you on a mate bond."

"Shut up." My words have no venom. They can all sense my new bond just as we know of Iosef's with his wife.

"He is good for you, 'Thina," Dimos says. "You do not hide yourself with him." My fleet's approval of him is important to me, but I'd still have chosen the bond if they didn't.

"I know."

The Drax soldiers still stand by. "Thanks for getting us here," Dejan says.

Dimos nods. An older soldier with an air of command steps forward. The Drax insignia is on his shoulder patch, and a large knife is strapped to his thigh.

"I'm Captain Bron Wolfe, commander of the Drax Guard. Thanks for getting my men back and for your help in the field."

Dimos presses a fist to his chest and introduces himself. Their words fade, along with the world around me, and Iosef catches me again.

"Steady."

I lean on him, desperate for anything solid amid this weightless feeling.

"I'd like an immediate debrief with everyone able to. Let's get her downstairs to get checked over." Captain Wolfe's tone doesn't really leave room for argument.

A female in scrubs and white jacket comes forward, her vibrant grey eyes friendly under a rim of kohl. Purple streaks her hair pulled back in a neat braid, showing the trim points to her ears.

"Come on with me." The fae beckons. My fleet pushes reassurance again. I stumble forward, grateful I don't have to sit through a debrief.

"I'm Cat, a resident at this hospital."

"Athina," I grunt back, leaning on the stair rail as we make our way down.

"Okay, Athina. Any significant injury I should know about first?"

"I don't think so." The stairs level out into a corridor with fluorescent lights. Some other nurses and white-jacketed doctors pass us. A few of the civilians stare in surprise at my beaten appearance.

Cat finally directs me into a room and to sit on the bed. After a cursory check and some mumbled answers from me, she ushers me into the washroom.

"Get started on a shower. I'll bring some clean clothes for you, and then we'll get to bandages."

I nod, but she's already gone. A haggard and filthy face stares back at me from the mirror above the sink. Chunks of hair have fallen from my once-tight braid. Red circles my neck from the silver collar. I wince just looking at the damage.

When the shower is filled with steam, I strip off filthy clothes and boots and step in. Heat bites into every scrape and bruise, water pressure scuffing at the sore muscles in my back. I could stay here forever, but there's the promise of medicine and clean clothes. Maybe a gallon of clean water. And I need to find Cieran.

When I step out and towel off, a stack of clean clothes awaits. It's grey sweatpants and a light blue T-shirt, and they fit decently.

Cat waits in the room, leaning against the wall beside a cart full of supplies when I finish dressing. I take a seat again and let her get to work.

There's some magic mixed in with the medicine she gives me to drink and the salve she spreads over my skin with how quickly the pain fades. She's quick and careful with the bandages, then fills out a band with information from me and my ident tags. It's carefully fastened around my wrist above the bond dampener. Cat leaves me with a smile and information that this is my room for the time being and they'll want to keep me for some observation.

Quiet lingers in her wake. My fingers spin the copper-inlaid bracelet around my wrist. Thanks to it, there's only a faint feeling of Cieran somewhere *out there.*

I slide my feet into the slipper-like shoes Cat also brought, and limp out into the hall. There's a nurse station ten feet down from my room and I walk that way. My loose hair leaves a damp spot on the back of my shirt, but my scalp aches too much to re-braid it yet. I feel exposed in the absence of anything familiar.

"Hey!" A human nurse at the station looks up from the stack of patient files to greet me. She wears a long-sleeved shirt covered in grinning ducks under her blue scrub top. The few other nurses glance over with friendly smiles from computers or more paper folders. It makes me feel a little more at ease.

"Hello." My voice is still a little hoarse. I need water. One of the nurses seems to sense this and puts a water bottle in front of me. I chug half of it while they wait patiently.

"Can I get some information on another patient, Cieran O'Donnell?"

The nurse types on her keyboard. "Your name?"

"Athina Spera."

Another round of typing. "What's your relation to him?"

"We have a heartbond." I lift my wrist to show the dampener bracelet.

The nurse lights up, but just as quickly sobers. "I will need someone to verify that. And I can't technically release info to you since you're not listed in his contacts." She smiles a little awkwardly at me. My lips tighten together. I'm not sure how to fight this.

"Athina!" Dejan's voice draws my attention before frustration can fully take hold. He and Remy stride down the hall, still in dirty gear and weapons.

"Hey." He leans on the counter, and the nurse gives a wide smile that the elf doesn't seem to notice. Dejan hands her a paper, and she scans over it. "Checking in on Cieran O'Donnell and Besim Antilles."

The nurse flicks a look at me. "Okay, this also verifies the heartbond. I'll make a note in the chart." She checks the screen. "Looks like they're finishing up with Cieran and will be moving him to a room, but that could be minutes or another hour." There's another apologetic shrug. "Besim is still in surgery, and there's not much else listed. Sorry."

"Cieran is all right?" I lean forward.

"The surgeons were able to fully re-knit his shoulder. They had to extract a bunch of residual magic and treat quite a few other injuries, but he's reported as stable."

My sigh of relief is matched by the others. When none of us make a move to leave, the nurse points down the hall. "There's a waiting area down there." She takes my water bottle, refills it, then hands it to me again with a smile.

I follow the others down the hall to where it flares into a rounded hallway intersection. Couches and armchairs made of fabric with abstract patterns are spaced out. A few low tables hold magazines or books. Remy takes a couch, setting his weapons down on the ground and shucking his pack. Dejan does the same in the armchair next to him and slouches into it. He takes off his hat, somehow still backwards this entire time, and drags a hand through his short blond hair. I wonder that weapons are allowed in a hospital but perhaps no one thinks to tell them "no."

I slowly lower into another chair to Dejan's left.

"Your crew is getting cleaned up and you'll have some quarters on base," Remy tells me. I nod my thanks.

"Who's calling Bes's family?" He digs out a phone from his pack.

"You don't want his mom to yell at you?" Dejan smirks a little.

"Not really."

"Come on, she likes you."

Remy shakes his head. "You have the higher rank."

I tilt my head. These two soldiers did not seem like they'd back away from anything.

"Don't mess with a woman who married a troll and had eight kids," Remy says. I huff slightly. Sounds like a formidable woman indeed.

"Fine, I'll do it." Dejan heaves himself up and pulls out his own device. "Call your people."

I tuck into the chair, bringing one foot up onto the cushion, trying not to listen in as they make calls.

Remy leans onto his knees, holding the phone in front of him to send a video to whoever will answer. He scrubs some dirt from his cheek, then runs his hand through thick, dark hair before the line connects.

"Hey, Bear." A genuine smile breaks across his face. A young boy shouts, "Dad!"

Dejan paces a few feet away, voice calm and soothing.

Dimos will send a message back to our headquarters and they will let our families know we are safe. Just hundreds of miles farther away than we'd ever planned. I hope he leaves out the heartbond. I want to be the one to tell my parents. Like I told Cieran, they won't mind he's human, and they will be pleased that he can stand next to me and not flinch.

Dejan flops back into the chair.

"You survived?" I ask.

He gives his sardonic little smile. "Yeah. We've got probably twenty minutes before Besim's parents and siblings descend and cause mass chaos."

The elf makes no other move to call anyone, and I wonder at it. But don't dare ask if there is anyone outside the hospital waiting to hear from him.

"Does Cieran have anyone else?" I ask instead, the words soft.

Dejan shrugs. "There might be someone else in his personnel file. CO will take care of it if there is."

"But likely not?"

He shakes his head again, teeth snagging at his bottom lip. The elf stares off across the waiting area. It seems like he's not quite with us anymore. I try to relax into the chair, maybe let my eyes shut for a moment, but every footstep or creak of wheels pulls my attention as I hope for news about Cieran.

Remy eventually puts away his phone, and the two soldiers fall to talking softly. A security guard passes by, looks at their weapons, then sees the insignia on their sleeve.

Perhaps it is not uncommon for Drax guards to be sitting in a waiting area. I spin the bracelet around and around my wrist, hating that I can't feel Cieran. My fleet doesn't say anything, but I can feel their bits of sympathy through the mindspeak as I sit here.

Finally, the nurse from the station finds us. Her ready smile allays some of my immediate fear at her approach. "They're getting Cieran in a room right now. Besim is still in with the surgeons, but they said it's looking good."

We release a collective breath. I stand up first as she waves us to follow, and we pause outside the door at her command. She steps in first. I listen intently for any sign of him.

"Hey." Cieran's tired voice sounds and my heart thuds hard in relief.

"Back again, Sergeant?" Her voice has a teasing edge.

"Just can't stay away, even if the food sucks."

She laughs. "I'd say use the suggestion box, but most of yours aren't appropriate."

There's something like a laugh from him. "I had some good ones."

"We're still not firing Dr. Pedoski or doing daily happy hour."

I shake my head, not the least surprised he would have done something like that. The crew exchange slight smiles.

"People'd be a lot happier if you did."

She chuckles again. There are a few beeps. "You've got some visitors if you're up for it."

He must have nodded, because the nurse steps into view of the door and beckons us in. Dejan ushers me forward and I tentatively step in, half afraid of what I'm going to see since the bond has been muted.

He's awake, the bed angled to prop him up slightly. IVs run from his arm to the machines. Cieran gives me a lopsided smile in bruised and swollen face. There's no reaction from the suppressed heartbond, just my own emotion stirring at the sight of him awake. His gaze slides past me to the crew.

"Hey."

"You look like crap," Remy says.

"That's just my face."

They grin. Drugs are likely obscuring some things for him, but he seems so relieved to see them.

"Besim?" he asks.

"The surgeons are still working, but it's looking good so far," Dejan reassures, looping thumbs around his tac vest straps.

"Good." The word sounds closer to pained. No one got left behind in the Wastelands this time.

"Rem got us to where your equipment was dumped. We got your stuff," the elf says.

Before Cieran can say anything, Remy speaks. "Dej picked up Javi's sword. The CO has it. He'll get it back to the family."

Brightness fills Cieran's eyes. Even with the dampener I can feel the relief and fresh burst of grief.

"Thanks." The word comes out thick.

"Get some rest, Sarge. We'll be around." Remy knocks a fist against Cieran's where it rests on the blankets.

Dejan does the same, then pulls the eternal hat out of the thigh pocket on his fatigues and sets it on the table. Cieran's gaze rests on the hat, then back to Dejan. The elf just tips his head. The crew give me nods as they file out, probably to go camp back out on the couches and wait for news on Besim. I step up to the bed.

"Hey, hot stuff," he says softly.

I shake my head, fighting a smile. "That one's sticking?"

"Think it might." A wince creases his features as he moves slightly. "You okay?"

"Yes. I've been cared for." I sit and slide my fingers through his. Bandages cover his neck, and lumps under the grey hospital shirt mark his other injuries.

"Hanging around?" There's a pained caution in his eyes.

I lean forward and gently kiss his forehead, reassuring that when he wakes, he won't be alone. "Think I might."

A sleepy smile swerves across his face. "Good."

Cieran's fingers tighten around mine before he shuts his eyes. His skin is warmer, and color is creeping back to his cheeks around the bruising. It doesn't look as bad as it should. The surgeons must have used as much magic as his body could handle to speed the healing process.

Cieran's eyes flicker behind his lids. He's not settling despite the medication pumping through the lines. My own exhaustion is about to fully ambush me, but I don't want to go down the hall to my room. "Move over."

One eye cracks open. He doesn't argue, only inches over, wincing as his shoulder jars. I softly apologize, and he just yawns in response. I curl up beside him on the bed, stealing a bit of pillow for my head, and rest my forehead against his shoulder.

My hand finds its way back into his and he tucks our hands atop his stomach. I inhale deeply, snuggling against him. "You smell better."

A muffled snort sounds. "Back at you."

I hum, letting my fire rise a little to combat the chill of the hospital room. Cieran sighs and pushes closer against me. Smiling, I let my eyes drift shut. His breath evens out. I let the sound reassure me, the feeling of safety overriding the potential embarrassment of anyone finding us like this.

We're both alive and together and ready to figure out this heartbond together.

22

CIERAN

BEEPING WAKES ME. I stir sluggishly, grimacing at the vaguely bitter smell of hospital antiseptic. I must have fallen asleep again at Shay's bedside. Either she's still asleep or she handed out death threats to the nurses not to wake me up because she somehow knows I didn't sleep last night.

When I will my eyes open, *I'm* the one lying in the bed and hooked up to lines and wires. My heart falls as memory filters in. Shay's gone, and I'm maybe in one piece after another trek out into the Wastelands.

Though something is missing. I turn my head, breath hissing through my teeth as bandages pull at my neck.

Athina.

She isn't curled up beside me anymore. The chair in the room is empty, and the only sound is the sporadic beeping from the machines. A brief inspection shows clear fluids being pumped in, probably some meds too by the way I feel a little groggy and my mouth is drier than cotton.

I sit up, huffing as muscles protest, and a warning stab comes through my left shoulder. Grit falls from my eyes as I scrape fingers across them. I'm about to try to stand up to loosen some of the tightness in my joints when a knock sounds. The nurse rounds the corner.

"You're awake! You've got some more visitors. They wanted me to see if you were up for it first."

More? Who would there be besides the crew and Athina?

My confusion must be leaking onto my face, because she says, "A Mrs. Moreno?"

The name hits the raw hole in my heart. But something in the last days has me finally brave enough to stand my ground. I nod, and the nurse steps out.

A dangerous mix of emotions well up at the sight of the woman peeking around the corner. Dark hair woven in a loose braid falls over her shoulder, her blue jacket bright against the white hospital walls.

"Hey, Cir." Javi's wife smiles at me, and I muster one in return.

"Hey. What are you doing here?"

Marisol fidgets with the purse strap across her chest. "Javi and I are still listed as emergency contacts in your file, along with Shay. They called me."

She trails off, the rest unsaid. Because the other two are probably marked as deceased. It leaves awkwardness between us. Maybe I can't do this.

Marisol steps closer. "You okay, Cir? What happened?"

I owe her something, a lot of things. Some of which have been finally knocked loose inside me over the last few days. Things I'm ready to offload and start living again.

"I got sent out to the Wastelands again."

She sucks in a breath, warm brown skin paling.

"It was supposed to be a routine mission. But we found...*him* alive."

Fury rises in her dark eyes. Although with a trace of fear. "And?"

"He's dead," I say flatly. "We got him."

Her jaw trembles and tears well in her eyes. She clears her throat and finds control again. "Good."

"Marisol." I pause. "I'm sorry for the last year. I just..." My hand rises and falls helplessly.

She sinks onto the edge of the bed. It must be raining outside since there's some drops on her jacket and spotting her jeans.

"Fates, I just miss them so much and I felt...hollow inside, and I couldn't face all of you, because I walked out and they didn't and..."

Marisol grabs me in a hug, much like the ones she'd give me when I'd stop by. We all had families and lives, but it didn't stop us from coming around between missions. "We don't blame you, Cir."

My vision blurs and I slowly hug her back.

"I'm glad you walked out, because that gives us some way to remember him, remember all of them."

"I've hated myself for fourteen months." The admission scrapes out.

Marisol pulls back, hands closing around mine. "Cieran, they wouldn't want you to. And I know if your and Javi's places were switched, he'd be in the same space. But I'd tell him to keep living, because you let them die again if you don't do anything to remember them."

"You think that'd go over well with Javi?" I arch an eyebrow.

She laughs softly. "Yeah, well, he'd admit I'm right after awhile. He always did, usually after you two beat the crap out of each other on the mats."

A chuckle bursts from me, and it's mixed with a sob. She rubs my arm. "I had to bring the kids with me. They're outside, but if you don't want them to come in, I understand. We brought some stuff for you."

I nod. "How terrible do I look?"

"Not too bad." She stands, plants a kiss on the top of my head, and steps outside. Rapid footsteps announce their two hooligans, and Joel and Tomás skid in.

"Uncle Cir!"

The title is a bit of a balm, and I don't have to fight for the grin.

"Hey!" I shift a leg to make room for their incursion onto the bed.

"What happened? Are you okay? Did you kill bad guys?" Their questions overlap.

"Slow down!" I laugh. "I need hugs first."

"Gently!" Marisol cuts in. She pulls up the chair to the side of the bed, smiling fondly at us.

Good thing she warned them, because the meds masked how tender my shoulder really is. My hand scrubs over their hair, and they both grin up at me, a bit of missing in the expression.

"Sorry I haven't been around recently."

The oldest sits back. Joel's five and he looks older than he should. "Mom said you were probably really sad about Dad and everyone."

His words gently tap my heart. "Yeah, I was. I miss them a lot."

The boys are quiet and Marisol dabs at her eyes.

"But." I clear my throat. "Maybe I could come around sometime and tell some stories about your dad and me."

"When?"

I lean closer and lower my voice. "I have to break out of here first."

"We can help." The newly four-year-old looks ready to pull a knife from somewhere and stealth out of here. Tomás looks so much like his dad, but it oddly doesn't sting.

"The doctors will tell him when he can leave," Marisol interrupts. "You want to give him your present?"

Tomás still looks ready to commit light arson, and I grin. Javi would be proud and would enlist me to help encourage him. Marisol clears her throat. There's warning in her slight smile like she knows exactly what I'm thinking.

They raid her purse and push brightly colored paper at me. I unfold one's pictures lopsided panels to reveal a fairly decent rendition of the crew in purple and green marker. Joel's handiwork.

"It's you and Dad and Uncle Masood and Uncle Marcel." Masood's beard reaches down to his chest and Marcel's mouth is a horizontal line. That part's accurate.

Another drawing gets shoved in my face. "And this is you with a tiger."

"I can tell." I grin at Tomás. I've no idea why he chose tiger. Maybe he'd been watching documentaries again, the little nerd.

"I'm going to put these on the fridge." I keep hold of them.

Marisol hands me a small square picture. "I was going through our wedding album a few days ago." She sniffs, but forges on. "That was one of the extras. I thought you might want it."

Javi and I in our dress uniforms grin out. We have arms slung around each other's shoulders, beers in hand. Other figures are blurs in the background.

"Thanks." I stare at it another moment, willing it to stay in focus.

"And there was another one I found." She hesitantly extends another one.

Shay had been my date to the wedding, and she'd killed it in a forest-green dress. It's a candid shot. I still had a beer in hand, but my head was tossed back in laughter. One of her arms was pressed over her stomach, face crinkled up in delight.

I catch the kids' wide eyes before I tip my head back with a deep breath. I've already cried too damn much recently, I don't really want to do it in front of the boys. But Marisol seems determined to make me.

"We all would have been there, Cir."

At the funeral. My throat cinches tight.

"Yeah." I don't have any words left to apologize for distancing myself, thinking I was alone in the world after Shay had gone. Too far trapped in my head to see the people I still have.

Small arms tackle me, not as gently as before, and little future-pyro is hugging me. I set my arms gently around him. Tomás scowls up at me. Maybe he's tired of all the tears too and just wants to remember the happy times.

"I ever tell you two about how your dad and I met?"

They hang around for the next hour, and the boys even convince me to show them my prosthetic. And I reluctantly admit that there is no knife storage inside, which would be a pretty sick idea.

Marisol starts to try to gather them up when a tentative knock sounds. My heart leaps back up at the sight of Athina hesitantly coming in.

"I don't want to interrupt." She directs it at me, but Marisol is honed in on her. With a faint sigh, I beckon Athina over.

"Marisol, this is Athina. She's a dragon shifter," I tell the boys. She gives a sort of awkward wave in response to their impressed stares.

"We...uh...met out in the Wastelands. Her crew was out there tracking...*him.*"

"And?" Marisol waits for me to get to the good part. I can see the light in her eyes.

My hand scrapes the back of my neck. "We have a heartbond." I rush through it fast, hoping she's not going to catch most of it. No such luck, as her grin stretches a mile wide.

"Oh, it is *so* good to meet you." She reaches across the bed to shake Athina's hand. Athina looks to me in slight confusion as she returns the greeting.

"This is Javi's family," I explain. Understanding lights her eyes, and she gives a little incline of her head.

"It is good to meet you as well."

"Did you know Dad?" Joel asks.

"Just what Cieran has told me. He seemed like a good man." Respect fills Athina's voice.

"Come over sometime and I'll pull out some of the good stories about the disasters these two got into with the rest of the crew." Marisol grins, and I know she's thinking about how epically the guys would have been roasting me this entire time.

"Don't worry. Crew Six has already been on top of it," I say wryly.

Marisol's laugh sparkles and it seems from the boys' expressions it's been awhile since it's echoed.

"You'd better let me know when you get discharged, Cieran." She starts gathering the boys in earnest. I get a couple more rib-crushing hugs, and Athina gets some waves.

"Will do."

They leave me still holding the pictures. Athina shyly sits down beside me. She's in sweats and a T-shirt. I have a vague memory of seeing her like that before.

"How are you feeling?" she asks.

"Slightly less pummeled."

Her smile twitches. "You look it."

Bandages still circle her neck and a few spot her arms. My fingers curl into my palm. All of a sudden I'm not sure how to act.

"You seemed happy to see them." She is blunt, but it's still refreshing.

"Yeah, I don't know...I think I finally got a look at something else out there." But she's all I'm focusing on. A bit of red tinges her cheeks. "And it's making me want to start pulling my way out of the pit I've felt stuck in."

Athina's warm hand wraps around mine. "I'm glad." Her thumb traces a pattern over mine. "You don't have to shoulder it all alone."

"I'm realizing that."

She smiles gently and turns to the pictures in my lap. I hand them over. Her smile grows as she takes in the drawings, then she sets them gently aside. Pauses longer over the photos.

"You clearly like beer."

I shake my head with a chuckle, and we fall into easier conversation. Now that death isn't hovering around the corner, and we're not avoiding a bond, we can actually get to know each other. We're both fiddling with the bond dampening bracelets, but the painkillers are starting to wear thin, and I don't want either of us to do something stupid again.

She's the one who finally reaches over and pointedly pushes the call button for the nurse. My frown holds no weight, and she knows it. She just steps aside for the nurse to start checking everything and then administer another dose of meds.

Athina stays, poking my good shoulder until I lie down. The combination of the medication and the lack of sleep over the last few days drag me back toward unconsciousness. I don't fight it, because this time I've got something better to wake up to.

23

Cieran

The next time I wake, it's not Athina sitting at my bedside, but a stocky elf with one boot propped up on the edge of the bed.

"Thought you were on mission," I say.

Ylan looks up from the magazine folded in his hands. "Technically I am, but figured my face was better than me and the boys sending flowers."

A faint grin tugs. "Is it too late to ask for flowers?"

He leans forward, propping elbows on knees, and smacks the rolled magazine against my prosthetic leg. "How you doing?"

"You heard?" I ask. If he's here, then Bron probably sent him a full update.

Ylan nods, face serious. "I answer my phone."

I roll my eyes.

After a moment, his laugh fades back to seriousness. "They'll rest easy now."

"Yeah," is about all I can manage before I lift a fist. "Thanks for being here."

He taps his fist against mine as he stands. "Glad you're back in one piece, Cir."

"Just tell me when you're coming over. I'll have some beer in the fridge," I say. He tucks his hands in his jacket pockets. I've missed the last few times he's come off mission, missed sharing a few beers and talking through some of it.

"You gonna answer if I call?"

I huff, but answer. "Yeah, came back a lot clearer."

Ylan tilts a faint smile. "Good. Sounds like there's a lot we need to catch up on."

"I'll be around."

He slides his hand out and clasps mine, holding for a second as we exchange a wordless goodbye. It's bad luck to say it, especially since he's headed back to the field. Back into dangerous undercover work.

"Tell them I say hi." I bump his fist one more time, then he backs away from the bed.

"Will do." Ylan offers another nod, glancing around like he's wistful he can't stay. But he's got a team to take care of and a mission to finish. We'll cross paths again.

I'm not alone for long before the nurse checks in. He frees me from the lines, and I get permission to get up and Besim's room number. I limp down the hall to look in on him. Athina's asleep somewhere close, just a comforting presence with the muted bond. I'll go find her later.

Besim's alone when I step in. I catch his empty, haunted stare at the window—an expression I know all too well—before he covers with a smile and a greeting.

He's got bandages across the left side of his face and down his left arm and hand. The surgeons are optimistic the burn scarring will be minimal since they got to him so fast. They were able to remove the last of the wild magic before it was too late.

He says it all lightly, but there's an edge underneath. So I pull up a chair and start talking, because he did the same for me in the Wastelands, and the absolute worst thing to be is alone in a hospital and covered in bandages.

It's not long before Dejan and Remy join us. They're both in street clothes and bearing paper bags filled with hot sandwiches for all of us from a small shop across the street from the hospital. For the rest of the afternoon, with all of us gathered around Besim's bed, we swap stories and I leave feeling a little lighter and like maybe I could find my way back to a crew. To this crew.

———

Four days later, the bond-dampener is removed. I'm given discharge papers and a warning not to come back and see them anytime soon. The clothes from my locker had been brought over along with my boots cleaned of Wastelands muck.

I make my way down to the first floor. Athina waits for me there and the heartbond gives a smug little thump. She's in fitted pants, her uniform boots laced up over. A plain shirt is tucked under a dark green jacket that hits just above her knees. The sleeves are rolled up her forearms. Her hair hangs in a loose braid over her shoulder.

I'm not the only one staring at her because she cuts a killer figure, something dangerous and calm all at once, but her focus is just on me. And I want to watch the way her lips curl in a smile forever.

I make my way over, claiming her hand. "Hey."

"Hi."

"Ready to get out of here?"

Athina pivots, exposing a knife hidden under the jacket. And I fall a little more in love with her. There's a lot we'll need to figure out, but that's something for another moment. Right now, I'm living inside this one, her hand in mine and a future beckoning.

"Where are we headed?"

There are a lot of places I want to take her. The house I've decided to keep, the top of the command tower to watch the sunset, other places that have some significance to me. But I have a promise to keep first.

"I know this great all-day breakfast place."

And we step out into the sunlight together.

The End

The Series Continues...

Faultline

Communications Specialist Besim Antilles has always felt invincible. As a half-troll with protective stoneskin that activates in a fight, he's never really taken a serious hit. Until a mission in the Allied American States Wastelands left scars all over his body, and a ragged faultline through his confidence.

When an elf sorcerer with ties to a terrorist organization Besim and his team have tussled with in the past shows up in his sister's coffee shop...let's just say he doesn't believe in coincidence.

Coffeeshop owner Nadire Antilles has two concerns—her fledgling coffee shop and her brother. He hasn't been the same since discharging from the hospital, and now he and his spec ops Drax Guard team are acting weird about some elf who came into her café. She trusts her brother and his team, but she also needs to keep the lights on so she doesn't lose her shot at the dream.

An open attack on the streets of Dunhare solidifies that the sorcerer is after the team. But as they race to find him and stop him for good, they discover he has a specific target in mind, and won't hesitate to draw Nadire right into the crossfire.

Read Now!

Acknowledgements

THESE ARE ALWAYS SO tough to start because there's always so much behind the scenes to produce a book, so many people, so many conversations, that sometimes it's hard to distill it all onto the page. But here we go.

This book started way back in 2021 as an attempt to break out of some intense mental and emotional burnout. It started handwritten in a notebook, and quickly got transferred over to the computer. It looked so different initially. Then the story kept coming. It wasn't until much, much later, after some friends had read the rough bones of the story that I got ideas for more books. I had fought free of burnout by then and was seized by the frantic excitement that was story ideas pouring in and the world expanding.

This series was briefly under contract with a publisher, and while it was heartbreaking to close that contract in 2023 before anything big happened in the publication process, that was for the best. This series needed space to breathe. I needed space to breathe. I needed space to develop the world and the characters. And come up with a few different potential spin-off series too. ;)

So thanks to Selina, Jenni, and Mollie who read the first iteration of this story and complained that I'd made them actually like a shifter romance. haha! What started out as an attempt to write a shifter romance in a slightly different way than the norm has become one of my favorite couples.

Thanks to Janeen Ippolito who helped guide me through my jump into urban fantasy and helped me build out the world. To Morlin Lorenz for the incredible character artwork and series logo. To Emilie Haney for knocking it out of the park with the covers!

Huge thanks to Jenni, Brigitte, and Laurel for reading the new version and flooding my inbox with messages and love for this book and characters.

And especially to Jenni, Brigitte, Mollie, and Gillian for the encouragement, support, the "pick yourself up off the ground, it's not terrible" talks. And just for being outstanding friends and an incredible support system.

Thanks to my family for being amazing and supportive. To my mom, who faithfully reads every book I write—sorry for keeping the *s* word in.

To my readers who've followed me through Scottish fantasy, Post-apocalyptic fantasy western, Nordic/prehistoric fantasy—thanks for jumping over to another new genre with me. I do hope you'll continue to hang out with these characters.

If you're a brand new reader—thanks for taking the chance on me and my book! It means the world to me. I hope you'll hop on for the ride.

And the biggest thanks to my Creator, without Whom any of this would be possible. The ideas, the ability to publish, the friends/support/readers. I pray always that the words I write will reflect His goodness.

Thanks for reading, and gear up. The missions aren't done yet.

MORE BOOKS BY C.M. BANSCHBACH

The Drifter Duology

LARAMIE WAS BORN TO ride the desert wilds. And she won't let anything stop her, even a fearsome war-lord who wants her captive–or dead.

A genius mechanic–and a rare descendant of the once magical Itan–Laramie drifts from dusty town to dusty town in search of the family that was taken from her.

But her rambling desert journey becomes a game of survival when Laramie crosses a ruthless warlord's territory. Taken prisoner by one of the warlord's biker gangs, she befriends a quiet, dangerous man named Gered. After surviving hellish circumstances Gered is tired of fighting for a better life.

Laramie will always fight. And she'll stop at nothing to win their freedom.

Enjoy this pulse-pounding motorcycle adventure in a post-apocalyptic western setting with found family and being brave in brutal circumstances. Complete series available!

The Spirits' Valley Duology

A man born for war. A bastard raised in contempt. Only together can they defend their tribe from slaughter.

Fierce-hearted Comran is the chief's son and the favored choice to be the next leader. Then his father chooses Comran's half-brother Etran for the role, straining the loyalties of the tribe and reinforcing the distance between the two men. When Comran is offered the role of battlewolf, he is ready to do his duty—but expects no friendship in return.

Steady Etran has long been shunned as the chief's bastard. Becoming the chief brings even more hostility, so he offers Comran the title of battlewolf to maintain tribal unity. But can he trust this reckless warrior as his general when Comran has never stood by his side?

As tensions mount within the tribe, a traitorous act leads to war. Comran and Etran must overcome their inner demons and fight for their brotherhood before the Greywolves fall to their worst enemies.

Read now!

———

Subscribe to C.M. Banschbach's newsletter for free short stories and book/publishing updates!

About C.M. Banschbach

C.M. Banschbach is a native Texan and would make an excellent hobbit if she wasn't so tall. She's an overall dork, pizza addict, and fangirl. When not writing fantasy stories packed full of adventure and snark, she works as a pediatric Physical Therapist where she happily embraces the fact that she never actually has to grow up.

She writes clean YA/MG fantasy-adventure as Claire M. Banschbach.

Facebook – @cmbanschbach

Instagram – @cmbanschbach

Website (books and merch)– https://clairembanschbach.com/

Newsletter (routine updates and access to exclusive short stories)– https://c-m-banschbach.kit.com/0134a85703